ENTERING NEW TERRITORY

ENTERING NEW TERRITORY

DREAMS FOR A NEW LOS ANGELES

**WRITTEN BY THE STUDENTS
OF THEODORE ROOSEVELT HIGH SCHOOL**
WITH AN INTRODUCTION BY
LOS ANGELES MAYOR ANTONIO VILLARAIGOSA
IN CONJUNCTION WITH 826LA

826LA

COMMUNITY EDITORIAL BOARD
Oscar Garza, Marita Forney, Dean Kuipers, Genevieve Leone,
Deborah Lowe, Tami Mnoian, Pilar Perez, Jacob Strunk,
David L. Ulin, Deborah Vankin, Gail Wronsky

THEODORE ROOSEVELT HIGH SCHOOL STUDENT EDITORIAL BOARD
Gabriela Bautista, Viridiana Bernal, Erik Estevez, Jennifer Guerra,
Eduardo Hernandez, Minerva Henriquez, Evelyn Martinez, Arnold Prieto,
Marisol Salgado, Madelyn Tapia

Entering New Territory

Published 2006 by 826LA

© 2006 All rights reserved by the authors and 826LA
ISBN 0-9768467-1-3

First Edition

826LA
SPARC Building
685 Venice Blvd.
Venice, CA 90291
(310) 305-8418
www.826la.org

Design: Michele Perez
Copy Editor: Sherri Schottlaender
Photographs: Anne Fishbein

This book was made possible with a generous donation from Max Palevsky and Jodie Evans.

Printed in Canada by WestCan P.G.

CONTENTS

INTRODUCTION:
DREAM WITH ME LOS ANGELES   *Mayor Antonio R. Villaraigosa*   11

THE STARS OF L.A.   *Issamar Camacho*   16

OF MY L.A.   *Eduardo Hernandez*   18

CHANGE THE WORLD   *Madelyn Tapia*   19

FEELING AT HOME   *Marisol Salgado*   24

LIFE'S DISILLUSIONS AND NEW HOPES   *Carina Lopez*   27

IN AND OUT OF THE PROJECTS   *Gabriela Fonseca*   30

RUNNING   *Juan Rodriguez*   33

M & M: BUDDIES, SISTERS   *Madeline Salazar*   38

HALF-INDIAN, BUT FULL LATINA   *Minerva Henriquez*   42

OPPOSITES ATTRACT   *Ana Rios*   47

A NURSE'S LIFE   *Keren Hernandez*   54

EAST L.A.: MY 'HOOD, MY HOME, MY HEART   *Wendy Rodriguez*   56

AN ODD DAY	*Dimas Ortiz*	59
LIKE A RACE	*Edwin Cervantes*	61
LOS ANGELES THROUGH MY EYES	*Hector Rodriguez*	62
THE BATTLE	*Jackeline Martinez*	64
THE TURNS IN LIFE	*Evelyn Martinez*	66
WHEN HE PICKED ME UP	*Jessica Juarez*	73
LONG WAY HOME	*David Blancarte*	76
EXPLORING L.A.: IN AND OUT	*Fabiola Avila*	80
ACQUAINTANCE	*Edgar Contreras*	82
LUZ ELENA, GHOST STORY TELLER	*Gabriela Bautista*	95
QUIETLY WISHING	*Esperanza Mendez*	99
THE OTHER PIECE OF MY LIFE	*Patricia Mendez*	103
MY VIOLIN DREAM	*Maria Sanchez*	107
I DREAM	*Rosalinda Rocha*	109
A WAY TO DREAM	*Kristopher Escajeda*	111
NAKED EYES	*Cristina Correa*	113
MY BROWN EYES	*Alexander Amador*	114
WALKING, TALKING, AND THINKING	*Arnold Prieto*	116

A CAR: A MUST-HAVE FOR TEENS IN L.A.   *Alejandro Rosales*   121

BUS BUDDIES   *Lady Sepulveda*   124

BLACK SHEEP?   *Viridiana Bernal*   127

THE GOOD IN EVERYTHING   *Jennifer Guerra*   129

JOURNAL ENTRIES   *Yvette Moreno*   138

DREAM DANCE   *Jackelyn Gomez*   140

THE SILVER LINING   *Christian Oliva*   142

'TIL YOU COME HOME, WE'LL BE WAITING   *Stephanie Velazquez*   149

HURT   *Erik Estevez*   151

DEAR MAYOR   *Julissa Acosta*   163

ABOUT THE AUTHORS   167

SOME WHO HELPED WITH THIS BOOK   172

ACKNOWLEDGMENTS   174

Mayor Antonio Villaraigosa with Roosevelt High student Erik Estevez

DREAM WITH ME LOS ANGELES
MAYOR ANTONIO R. VILLARAIGOSA

I was incredibly honored when I was asked by Pilar Perez, the fantastic executive director of 826LA, to write the introduction to this book. It meant so much to me because I am a graduate of Roosevelt High School, and this text is a terrific symbol of my high school experience coming full circle. I know that the future mayor of Los Angeles is sitting in a classroom at Roosevelt right now, but that child needs the help and support of all us to make sure that he/she achieves his/her goals.

The people of my hometown have honored me by electing me mayor of the cultural and entertainment capital of the world: Los Angeles. Although I am fortunate to be in the position I am in today, I will never forget where I came from. For me, the path from City Terrace to City Hall ran directly through Roosevelt High School. While that may seem like a short trip, we all know what a vast distance it truly is—it's a distance that can't be measured in miles or calculated in terms of the achievements of any one person.

I am here today because of the indomitable spirit and boundless faith of my mother, Natalia Delgado, a woman who struggled as a single mom, sometimes working two jobs to put my siblings and me through college. On the day I was elected mayor, I remarked that if my mother had been with me, she'd have said, with that vision of a better future still gleaming in her mind's eye, "Antonio, don't declare victory tonight—declare your purpose."

Although I grew up in a home where there was not a lot of money, it was a rich place both culturally and spiritually. I still remember sitting with my family in the living room as my mother read Shakespeare, Keats, and Hemingway to us. Despite the fact that my mother provided a tremendous foundation for me during my childhood, I still stumbled, at times, along the way. I struggled at various points in my youth, but my mother never let me use the fact that I grew up in a single-parent household and saw alcoholism and domestic violence firsthand as an excuse to fall behind.

My journey also ran through the night school classroom of an exceptional teacher named Herman Katz. Mr. Katz saw something in me that I didn't even see in myself at the time. He helped me to refocus on what my priorities needed to be—mainly, getting a good education—so that I could go forward and succeed. Mr. Katz took me under his wing, tutored me after school, and even helped pay for me to take the SAT exam so that I could go to college.

I know the feeling that many children at times experience in Los Angeles: for many reasons, they feel a sense of hopelessness. For me, the knowledge that my mother and Herman Katz instilled in me was crucial to my completing high school and moving on to UCLA. They both taught me to never give up my dreams.

There are a series of towers that rise over Watts that are an example of what you can achieve when you dream. The Watts Towers, built by the Italian artist and immigrant Simon Rodia, were a thirty-three-year labor of love. Although Rodia used simple tools and cast-off materials in their construction, for more than half a century the Watts Towers have remained standing. They've withstood natural and man-made catastrophes, surviving despite the efforts of critics, the ravages of earthquakes, and the proximity of civil unrest.

Seen from afar, the Watts Towers rise like the spires of a great cathedral, but up close, you are immediately drawn in by the amazing complexity of their design. Embedded in those walls and spires are thousands of cast-off objects representing every imaginable color and shape and texture and form. They're made from bed frames and bottles and broken glass, from scrap metal, pot shards, and ceramic tiles. When I see those towers soaring over Watts, my thoughts always return to all of the individual pieces that make up that beautiful whole; to the value in those things that people, in their haste, are apt to cast away; to the awesome power of disparate elements working together to achieve such dazzling harmony. Simon Rodia was asked late in his life to explain the meaning of his work, and he offered this simple reply: "I had in mind to do something big, and I did it."

Simon Rodia was asked late in his life to explain the meaning of his work, and he offered this simple reply: "I had in mind to do something big, and I did it." Let's heed Mr. Rodia's words. Let's do something big for Los Angeles. Let's raise our eyes skyward. Let's imagine the pinnacles that we can reach together—all of us, without regard to race or geography or language, without regard to age or religion or gender or sexual orientation. Let's dare to dream. Let's dare to dream together.

I would like to thank Cecilia Quemada, the fabulous principal at Roosevelt High School. I'd also like to extend thanks to Pilar Perez, the executive director of 826LA; Deborah Lowe, Marita Forney, and Estelle Ost, teachers at Roosevelt; and Amber Early and all of the 826LA tutors. They are inspirations to us all. Most importantly, I'd like to thank the students of Roosevelt High School who had both the courage and dedication to participate in this book and share a piece of themselves with us all. You are the true heroes. Never stop dreaming.

THE STARS OF L.A.
ISSAMAR CAMACHO

I know the power of the youth is there . . .
Like stars
struggling to shine through,
But poisonous smog conceals the sky
with a stifling façade.
We are constantly worrying about
being stopped in the street
by the cops for being brown,
attending school with prison gates,
learning from the same books our parents
used in their classes:
decaying, outdated
          . . . insulting.
Constantly being told that only a few
of us can make it: *only by selling out your people*
can you be successful . . .

The smog veils the stars' true purpose   with a soft grin;
(Allowing a few stars to shine through
in order to not be discovered).
It will not be l o n g until the stars
become conscious of the
deception.

They will not doubt their strength any longer;
waking up at 5:00 in the morning
to catch the bus
and get to a class of 43 in order to learn;
having a job while still in school
in order to help support the family;
concentrating on their future

even though they are constantly told they will fail;
and too often worrying about someone in
their family being deported—
including themselves . . .
knowing that if they make it to college
they will be expected to carry all of their people
on their shoulders.
They will understand their **power!**
Relentless in the struggle against the obstructions.

OF MY L.A.
EDUARDO HERNANDEZ

The carroty apartment I used to subsist in
The citrus-scented floor oil I used to smell
The toasty warm times I used to spend in bed
Hot chocolate in the cold first light

The lime green FRIENDLY MARKET
I called "Los Chinitos" across the street
The tacos I used to eat from El Cremas
The lofty trees that blocked the dazzling sun

The radish-tinted LOS RAMIREZ
Which I called "Los Mexicanos"
The sticky concrete which when I
Stepped on it gave me shivers

The old FINES FOOD MARKET with the
Smell of fresh steamy out-of-the-oven bread
The old VHS movie rental store
With the smell of cool fluorescent fruits

The old SEARS which had no S
Which at night spelled EARS
The cold rich ice cream they sold
And the sugary vanilla savory churros

My life has changed because I have moved
To a pink tiny house which I call Pink Panther
No more places to go without a car
Houses everywhere but no one in sight

The sense of loneliness

CHANGE THE WORLD
MADELYN TAPIA

The smell of exhaust seeped in through the etched-on windows.
The words as I moved
Spun webs
Connected by black widows.
Water
       Dripped
             Dripped
                   Dripped
Endlessly;
The rain,
The wind
       —Awarding inadequate samples of clean, fresh air
      In an enclosed vehicle.
Unfortunately, not reaching the back of the Metro
Where I had been seated
Crowded by sweaty people,
      Like the man
Holding the pole,
     A sickle
          Holding tighter,
So as not to fall
When the bus abruptly brakes.
But the man had fallen
         Stumbled
"For God's sake!"
She yelled, disgusted
Moving out of his way,
         Letting him F
           A
           L
           L.

The stink of alcohol, cigarettes, sweat
    Completely made my skin crawl.
His feet
    Stunk of exotic cheeses.
Suddenly I thought,
    While craving Reese's Pieces,
This dirty man is at my shoes.
Absorbed was I with his life, his dues.
A feeling within had arisen
    Depressing my heart.

How could this have happened to this man—how did it start?

Wake up!
Knock at the door
The sheriff,
A sign,
We all know what it's for
"Sir, I'm sorry, but you need to leave the premises."
"*Y mis hijos?* Where are we supposed to go?"
"You should have paid, sir."
The sad look,
Their faces.

Ten years working at that factory and what do I have to show for it?

"They" fired me for being incompetent,
Although I worked harder than the rest.
"They" fired me for being an immigrant,
Because I complained about our pay.

My hand,
Coarse,
Dark mocha.
My daughter,
Hazel-green eyes,
Dark brown hair.
Suddenly
Running far

Seeing if my life could be found.

So many problems, no one seems to care.

The sky, I am falling
I stop,
I am crawling.
Reeking of beer,
Unstable
Caught in this never-ending fable.

I see a bus,
Start running.
Inside the bus. "Made it."
Empty pockets, but still. "A dollar twenty-five."
The driver,
His blue uniform.
He says, "Sir, I mean it."
Feel so beat up,
Searching for "a dollar twenty-five."

Next stop,
A girl
Light-brown eyes.
"Don't worry,
I'll pay." She had a nice voice.
"*Gracias, Señorita,* ju ahr so nice."

So I am in the midsection of this moving ride.
Hands, slippery
Head, pulse-aching.
The
Smell

Awful,
And I want to hide,

Get off
The bus of criticism,
They all listen,
Contemplating.

"Do the riders, all those who stare,
Do they know who I am, truly?
Do they even care?"

A thought,
Only a thought,
No one,
No one
Can see.
Everyone sees the surface,
The cover,
No one reads the book.

Suddenly a slip,
I fell.
I fell again.
Fell once again, the man who saw hell.
Look up to see my daughter,
Not my daughter,
Another man's daughter, who looks like her
My little angel, my life, the one I miss.
"Why does she stare at me?"

Is he drunk? Should I help him up?

"Can she see me?"

The man ran out, ran out crying.
I don't believe he was drunk.

If I said, "I do not care at all," I would be lying.

My stop,
Pull the cord,
    The driver brakes.
Shy as she is she must do what it takes.
She has the speech ready
            Entitled "Whatever It Takes."

For "They" have judged us so cruelly.
But soon
    All will see
How instrumental we can be.
      Change the world.
        Move her forward.
No more violence—
Whatever it takes to end the silence.
The students, the children, will be heard.

We will	*Nous venons*	*Nosotros vamos*
Change the world.	*Changer le monde.*	*A cambiar el mundo.*

Bit by bit.

FEELING AT HOME
MARISOL SALGADO

Daniela was running down the congested street. There were many people bustling around, trying to get home to their families; it had been a long week for everyone. Daniela was exhausted and her legs were numb from swimming practice. She was a responsible person, and in order to prove that to her mom, she had to get home quickly to clean the small, cozy apartment to which she had recently moved.

As Daniela was dashing home, she stopped at a crosswalk and noticed a bus stop crowded with people. The people looked impatient and worn out. One thing in particular caught her eye: a man in a wheelchair was struggling to get in the bus, as the driver stared at him impatiently. This incident made her think about Santa Ana, where she used to live before moving to L.A. five months earlier. In Santa Ana, the bus drivers were more sympathetic.

Daniela was approaching her house. As she walked up the stairs towards the front door, she saw her neighbor. They made eye contact and Daniela smiled at her, but the neighbor ignored her and walked right by. Daniela thought about how warm her neighbors were back in Santa Ana.

She opened the front door of her house and the smell of spaghetti went up through her nostrils, dropping into her stomach like an atomic bomb. Her mom was cooking while her younger brother Frank sat in the living room doing his homework. When they each finished with their responsibilities, they sat down to the table to have dinner, just the three of them.

While scrubbing the dishes, Daniela realized that not only did she have to come to terms with her move from Santa Ana to L.A., but she also had to accept living in a house with a man she hardly knew. Later that day, while she was inside her modest room watching TV with her brother, she heard the door open. It was her stepfather, all dressed in white, with paint all over his face and on his grayish hair. One look from him filled them with a kind of dread. As always, Daniela and Frank feared the unknown.

The day ended with a simple "good night," and Daniela went to bed wondering what might happen the next day. Her life was going to change.

Early Saturday morning Daniela woke up to the slam of a door; it was her stepfather going to work at 6AM. She lay in her bed, relieved that he was gone. She got up and went out to the living room, where she found her mom dressed and ready. Her mom announced, "We are going to Santa Ana." Daniela became excited once she heard the words "Santa Ana" leave her mom's heart-shaped lips. She quickly helped her mom make scrambled eggs as the bacon sizzled on the stove. They ate breakfast together like a blissful little family. As soon as they finished, they left for the place they used to call home.

The moment her mom drove into Santa Ana, Daniela felt butterflies in her stomach. She couldn't wait to be reunited with her aunt and cousins. Once she opened her aunt's front door, she felt her world spinning with excitement. The whole family went to Centennial Park, not far away from her aunt's happy home; at the park they had a small barbeque and played baseball. She felt overjoyed being there in Santa Ana, in the park, with her family.

The time to return to L.A. soon drew near, and Daniela felt heartbroken. As soon as they got home, she and her mom rushed to prepare dinner for her stepfather. Daniela then went to her room to play Monopoly with Frank—she didn't want to eat with her stepfather. She couldn't fight the fear of the unknown.

Daniela was about to role the dice when she heard the front door slam hard, harder than usual. She felt chills throughout her body. The siblings looked at each other. They both knew what was about to happen. They silently closed their door and waited. Soon they could hear the arguing in the living room, then the screaming and crying began. Frank hid under the bed. Daniela felt powerless.

Daniela's mom dashed into their bedroom; she covered her face because she felt ashamed to cry in front of her children. Still, the tears were visible, rolling down her cheeks, and her eyes were red and puffy. Frank came out from under the bed and said, "Daniela, let's go try talking to him." Hearing those words come from her timid ten-year-old brother surprised her and gave her strength. She couldn't hide in fear any longer. It was the right thing to do—in fact, it was their only hope of making a better life in L.A. for all of them.

Frank and Daniela went outside to confront their stepfather. They told him firmly how they had sacrificed everything: they had moved to

L.A. in order for their mom to be happy. They told him they were willing to get along with him. He was a man who could become an important person in their lives; if he would only try to be a true dad, he might become the only father they had ever known. Finally, he began to soften. He looked at them with tears in his eyes.

Now Daniela could begin to call Los Angeles her new home. Deep in the heart of the city, she finally found her family.

LIFE'S DISILLUSIONS AND NEW HOPES
CARINA LOPEZ

As a kid, you just want to be happy. You want to be with the people who care for you and who you care for, because you love each other. You want to feel good with your family. Kids want to live with peace and love and think that everything makes sense, that people are actually kind, and that everything is OK. When I was an infant my happiness was infinite, and I was overflowing with joy. I was happy from kindergarten until elementary school, because I had a really giddy picture of life. I also had lots of dreams . . .

I thought for sure that one day I would be a star, a really great star. I would escape to my own world and dream. I thought that someone would discover me and notice the beauty inside me.

My grandma inspired me to dream, and she also motivated me to make those dreams fly. Dreams can actually happen if you have faith and believe in them wholeheartedly; if you're pessimistic, you won't get anywhere. Faith is what keeps all of us going and trying to get somewhere in life. The support and love of my grandma gave me what I needed. She and I would always have really fun times, especially when we traveled. I saw her as a divine being and always pictured us being together.

When we would travel to Acapulco, it was like we were in paradise. My grandma helped me to forget the troubles that were beginning to enter my life and to just live in the moment. We would laugh, discover, appreciate, and experience new things. Christmas with her was the best, filled with sensitivity, love, peace, harmony—rather than being materialistic or meaningless, everything was flooded with joyfulness.

My grandma was always there for me in good times and bad. She used to say that if you put your head, your heart, and your soul to something, you could do it. She was strict with me, but patient and loving. I was her little girl, her first granddaughter.

When I was about seven, I started spending more time with my parents. This was a really different experience: the picture I had of life moved from one path to another. I was happy to live with my parents because I thought that's how it's supposed to be, but when I began to understand the relationship between my mother and father, it made me feel frustrated. We were a crazy family. At times we could be really happy, but it would all turn into misery in minutes. My mother, brother, and I could be having a good time, then all of a sudden it would turn into silence because my father would come into the house drunk. All of my fatherly ideas about him turned into dust.

It was difficult to get in my head the idea that happiness doesn't last forever. As I witnessed how my family was becoming dysfunctional, I became emotionally drained. My father would go out and get drunk; he was living a life that would bring him nothing but misery. This was giving him a miserable image of life. My mother was always reserved and wouldn't speak up. She lived on her knees, letting everyone step on her. My father was one of them: he was not fair with her or with us, his children. He knew that what he was doing was not right, yet he was not mentally, physically, or spiritually able to stop it. My parents lived their lives arguing, even though they had feelings of love for one another.

I still saw my grandma from time to time, and I always remembered her encouragement to go for it and not have limits. I used to think that I would always have her around, but now I only saw her once in a while. Being away from my grandma from one day to another wasn't easy. Life has some really big turning points, and being apart from her was one for me. It felt like being on a roller coaster, with high and low points, from joy to frustration.

Without my grandma, I had nobody by my side anymore. Life can feel like a magical world, and then all of a sudden you wake up and realize it was all just a dream. You have to face the world and see how cruel it is. Maybe adults make it easy for you when you're little but go harder on you when you're older.

As I grew up, I saw that the world is not what I thought it was. Life is hard. I realized that my dreams were illusions and that my surroundings were not the best. Dreams can have wings, but when you break a wing, it is hard to repair it and keep on flying.

I started living with hope for a brighter future, seeing myself as a something and someone. Now I know that I am bright and that I can do anything I set my mind to; I even discovered that I have writing skills. I realized that I shouldn't be afraid of reality, because it is everywhere.

We all have to face our fears—I myself have done that. The thought of my family splitting up and being torn into pieces was horrible, but once you know there's no turning back, you have to face front. Even if you feel that there's no great support behind you, you should be determined. It is absurd to let yourself drown in a puddle when you haven't even gotten to the sea yet.

We all have to struggle to get to the top, but getting there is magnificent: a sea of glory awaits, where you shall feel triumphant. I am grateful for everything I've been through because it has made me strong and determined. I shall keep on climbing the stairway in L.A.—and never trip—'till I get to heaven.

IN AND OUT OF THE PROJECTS
GABRIELA FONSECA

I was sixteen years old when rumors started flying that the local police station was going to expand its facility. At first I didn't pay much attention, but as rumors began to spread, I became worried. Our neighbors were beginning to leave, and they told us it was because the city had bought the apartments they lived in; ours was the only property that had not yet been bought. Then my parents learned that the police station had bought our rental house, too. My dad said, "We need to start looking for a place."

"Don't worry; we still have a couple of months before we have to go," my mom said.

As they talked, I kept thinking about how I didn't want to move because I didn't want to leave my best friend, Rosa. I had known her since the sixth grade, and she was like a sister to me. So I did something that surprised even me: I started praying (or I thought I did, because I didn't know how to pray very well). I prayed that the city would decide not to expand the police station and that we wouldn't have to move, because if we did, it would wreck my life completely—or so I thought. That's how dramatic I was.

Of course, my prayers didn't come true, and soon my parents started to look for a new place. At the time I wasn't concerned with where they were looking, because my biggest concern was leaving Rosa. We were both very sad because we didn't want to part, but we both knew that we had to. In the weeks that followed, my dad came home every day to tell my mom about the apartments he found. They would both be really excited as they left to look at a new place and come back really frustrated because the deal was never as good as it seemed. They wouldn't discuss anything with me, and I was beginning to feel frustrated too—I wanted to know where they were looking for a house so I could tell my friend Rosa where *she* should tell *her* mom to look so that we could live close to one another again.

Then, one day my mom was talking on the phone with my aunt, and I heard her say the word "projects." That's when I realized they were going to look at apartments in the projects. I was shocked, because if you live in a nice house and then go to live in the projects, it's considered a step down: usually people moved *out* of the projects, not *into* them. Or that is how I saw it. I was full of negativity.

About three weeks later, my mom dropped the bomb: we *were* moving to the projects. I was scared and disappointed, because in my eyes they hadn't tried hard enough to look for a better place. After I heard the news, I told Rosa, "I'm moving to the projects." And she said, "No! I wouldn't go there. Its horrible. I've already lived there once." I was so frustrated because nothing was turning out as I wanted it to.

In December, we moved. I was angry about the whole thing. I was mad because I'd moved from a really nice, spacious house with a really big backyard—with one of my best friends as my neighbor—to a place with a yard I had to share with neighbors I didn't even know. And I didn't have any friends there. To top it all off, there was no space—the apartments were so close together they were like lockers at school. And there was no privacy at all. I could hear noise coming from the apartments on either side of us, and sometimes I felt like throwing a shoe at the wall so they would be quiet—but I didn't. The noise from the neighbors killed me; I could hear when they woke up because it was as if they were banging on the wall. It was especially annoying because they got up really early, and they would make even more noise on the weekends. Everything that happened in the projects annoyed me. I hated the whole thing.

Everything changed that first Christmas season. The whole community came together at a specific house, and the host provided food. This Mexican tradition is called a posada, so it was not new to me, but I was surprised that it would occur in the projects. At that point I began asking myself if the rumors I had heard about the gang members and drug dealing in the projects were true or just exaggerated stories. That Christmas, my concept of the projects changed as I saw families just like mine, with the same values, background, and culture; for the first time, I identified with the families living there. I began to see that some really cute guys lived there too, so that helped a lot. Soon I discovered that some sweet little girls lived next door to me, and I really liked talking with them.

(I haven't written about my brothers because this essay is supposed to be about me, but I'll tell you a bit about them anyway. I have an eight-year-old brother who was sad when we moved, because he was leaving his friends behind as well. He totally forgot about them, though, when he met Georgina, our new next-door neighbor, who he really bonded with. I have another brother who is three, so the move didn't really affect him.)

Well, back to me. During the nine months that I lived in the projects, I bonded with my cousin Kenia, who also lived in the projects. I hadn't talked to her that much before we moved, but I found out that she was really fun to be around; she would come to my house and we'd chat about boys, and I felt less alone. I also met a girl who reminded me of Rosa, and so I could relate to her. We would talk about boys and things we did with our friends, and it was quite fun, because sometimes we would stay outside until it got really late and one of us was called inside.

Then, at the end of September I found out that we were moving again—and I was mad, because I had already gotten attached to the place. I kept thinking that if we had moved during the first months that we were there, it wouldn't have mattered, but now I was attached. I didn't want to move, but on October first we left. It's ironic: at first I hated the projects, but now that I'm gone I actually miss living there.

I've moved three times, and each place that I've lived has something that makes it special. In my first house I felt really safe because I had the police station nearby. In the projects I didn't feel at all safe, but it gave me a sense of warmth; it was a place where I could relate to the people around me and experience my culture a little bit more. I also learned to accept how other people live during the nine months I was there. And Rosa and I are still good friends—even though we are separated and live really far away from one another's houses, we've managed to stay in touch.

My dream for L.A. is that people get to experience a sense of security within their own communities and are able to further explore their culture, like I did, and find a community that embraces them.

RUNNING
JUAN RODRIGUEZ

It's a Sunday night, and I am watching a sports film that makes me reflect about my own experience as a runner. My mind begins to wander, and I dream about the many things I have seen throughout my three years of running through the streets of Los Angeles. I feel fortunate that I have had the opportunity to run many distances, from one to eighteen miles. I have seen what represents Los Angeles to me: the Hollywood Sign high up on the mountainside; the coyotes and me, scared of each other. By Elysian Park, near Dodger Stadium, I can hear the fans being rowdy. In Griffith Park I can see marathon runners, cross-country runners, and ultra-runners from different parts of the world. And finally, there's the L.A. Coliseum, where the Raiders used to play. I feel sad that L.A. doesn't have a football team to cheer for—I imagine the Raiders and the Packers tackling each other on the field.

I finish eating a bowl of spaghetti because that's all there was to eat in the house. I continue watching TV, a biography of a famous runner, a legend: Emil Zátopek. He holds eighteen world records—he is known for starting speed work while at the same time running long distances. His teammates thought he was crazy; they didn't think speed work would help a long-distance runner. Though the concept of speed work is foreign to many, it worked for me as well as it did for him. By making my muscles stronger, it protects the muscles from cramping up and getting injured. It's like stretching!

I start to doze and dream about running in Los Angeles. I find myself outside my house with my new running shoes. They're Asics, red with white stripes that curve and cross each other. I start heading down the stairs and open the gate and head down the dirty alley . . .

Boyle Heights

I run down Mott Street, where my house is located. I pass a delicate flower garden that is roped off in the shape of a rectangle in front of my friend's house, which is the only place that has flowers on the whole block. The flowers are well maintained, sitting in the middle of the concrete. The soil is rich and soft. Some people in the neighborhood have fake gardens, but this isn't one of them. The flowers are about three feet high, dark red, and have already blossomed. The rest of the block is filled with grime and trash.

While I run towards Hollenbeck Middle School, I notice a mountain of soil next to the campus. When it rains, the dirt and plants slide onto the sidewalk. The plants, which remind me of the kind that are used to make shampoo, are ruined by the mini-avalanche. The soil is dark brown and looks like it's always wet, as if it could produce plants faster than any other land. I cross the street and run to Roosevelt High School, which is 500 meters bigger than Hollenbeck. I run up to the corner of Fourth Street and Mott—it takes me about a minute and a half. I turn left and can see the inside of Roosevelt, the track, football field, the tennis courts, and the pool. Then I pass a small barbershop. Inside, the kids get haircuts and talk about sports and girls. There's a store next to the barbershop; it's a miniature shop that sells meat. I have to squeeze in between boxes of tomatoes and the refrigerator to find the candy counter. I grab a bottle of Mountain Blast Gatorade. It's the best flavor because it feels fresh as the mountain air in the morning. I pay for it and leave the store, heading towards Soto Street.

I see a supermarket next to a gasoline station. There aren't many cars parked outside the market. Everybody is at work, but there are still many people getting gas on their way to work. People work hard in this neighborhood. They're always moving, even at six o'clock in the morning. I notice there is an abundance of little restaurants and donut shops; they are empty. I keep on running down the hill and get to Hollenbeck Park. The park is more than one mile long; there's a playground with new swings and slides, which is surrounded by black fences with sharp spikes to protect them. Next to the playground, there's a dirty greenish lake where you can fish—you can't eat what you catch there, so most people just throw their fish back in the water. Many ducks surround the lake. They wobble up the hills and into the water. They don't look happy—maybe because it's so polluted. Not only do people carelessly throw cans and bottles into it, but they even throw in shopping carts. One day, I remember on the morning news hearing that they also found a car in the lake. No one knew how it got there.

The park is a grand place to practice cross-country running because it has several grassy hills. Running into the park, I pass the lake and the playground. By the time I emerge from the other side, the sidewalk becomes bumpy and destroyed. I trip and wake up to find myself on the floor—I'm suddenly at home in my room. My throat is dry. I hear the sound of the TV. The movie has ended, and now *M*A*S*H* is on. I put my blankets onto the bed, turn off the TV, and try to go back to sleep. Suddenly, my Ama comes into my room and forcefully says, *"Pense que te dije que te fueras a dormir hace una hora."* I exclaim, *"Horita, cierre la puerta!"* So I try to go back to sleep, but I can't. I turn on the lights and start reading a book called *Track and Field: The East German Textbook of Athletics*, by Gerhardt Schmolinsky. I start to drift again, my eyesight goes blurry . . .

Downtown

I am running through downtown and notice the ground is sticky with gum and soda. There are tents of a greenish guacamole color, ripped in different places, where I see the homeless sleeping, shivering like wet dogs. Near the tents are cardboard boxes folded on the ground and rusted shopping carts that have empty bottles, cans, blankets, and broken-down radios in them.

The faces of the homeless are hidden by their long hair and unkempt beards. Their faces and clothes are sticky and faded because it seems they haven't taken a shower in ages. Their unwashed clothes are ripped in different places, like in the knees, bottom of the pants, and in the behind. Many of them are walking slowly, like snails. They ask people passing by for change. It's impossible to understand them because they're mumbling to themselves. I reach the heart of Downtown and see what is so alluring about the city: the different cultures; browsing through the stores; and people on their way to work. The city contains many jewelry stores, fast food restaurants, law offices, toy stores, and rug stores. There's every kind of store you can imagine. There's a construction site next to the shops and restaurants and I am not able to run, but before I can react, I fall in a sewer that was opened up by one of the construction workers. I wake up and once again I am on the floor of my bedroom with my book on the ground next to my track shoes. I stand up and pick up my blankets, turn on the lights, and walk to the kitchen and get myself a glass of water. My throat is dry. I drink another glass and pick up the book again to start reading until I doze off.

Griffith Park

When I finally get into a deep sleep, I find myself running towards Griffith Park, entering via Los Feliz Boulevard. Near the parking lot, some ponies are lazily standing still, unable to walk. Their eyes show their exhaustion from being taken from place to place. The ponies are white, brown, black, and spotted—they represent a different kind of diversity. The animals are chained and roped so they won't get away. I ask myself, why chain them if they can barely move? I keep running through the parking lot, by the train ride and the roller coaster. Next to the rides there's a food stand where they sell cotton candy, popcorn, and soft drinks. I want to ride the train, but I can't. I keep running. In the parking lot, there is oodles of human diversity. I start running on a little trail that lies straight ahead; it's about eight miles round-trip. I can see the 5 Freeway, and I notice cars rapidly speeding by. By six o'clock, there's a standstill. There's a straightaway that has a lot of trash strewn about because that's where they put the waste when they're reconstructing parts of the trail.

It's misty outside, and the air is fresh. It feels marvelous, and I think I can run forever. I pass by the golf course, and I see the freeway again. During the second mile, there's a dark, gloomy tunnel with a low echo. It seems as if it goes on forever even though it's only twenty to thirty meters long. When I get to the other side of the tunnel, I see people jogging in groups, and bike riders rushing by. I can see the L.A. Zoo where one can see different creatures of all kinds. I arrive at another tunnel, but it is closed. I enter it anyway, and all I see is darkness—I feel isolated and cut off from civilization. I blaze up into the mountains, which is a steady mile up. The fog and mist make me hesitate. I don't know where to go. Luckily, a water fountain appears. I take a sip of water that slightly refreshes my throat. I begin down a hill, and a sign forces me to change directions. Over my shoulder, the faraway city dreams, and a little lagoon, which seems like a dried-up dam, whispers, "I'm filthy. Run faster."

I turn left. Minutes go by. Running down the steep hill, I feel woozy. The hill gets steeper, and I feel lonely, I feel tired. I'm about to stop. The dirt turns into concrete. Runners appear out of nowhere. The mile feels like a battle. A big boulder appears—I turn left; I go down; I move straight ahead. The concrete road angles upward and it becomes really hard to run. I try to stop, but can't. I see Madonna's mansion. It looks like a church. Big garden. Beautiful. The Hollywood Sign looks huge. I feel dizzy. I'm falling. I'm yelling. Boom!

Finally, it's morning. I am sweating like a pig. I feel so tired. I get my sister's radio even though she tells me not to. I take it in the bathroom, connect it, and put on Latino 96.3. I take a bath and then put on my shorts and my Asics. I go down the stairs, open the door, and go down the alley. I turn left, go down Mott Street, and see . . .

M & M: BUDDIES, SISTERS
MADELINE SALAZAR

Los Angeles—the wild city where I was born and raised. In my fourteen years of life, I have encountered many things: Mr. O'Dell, the greatest English teacher; Mireya and Sonia, my friends; the people and the streets of my neighborhood. No matter what the situation, I have always faced it with courage, hope, and laughter.

I was never sure what my life would be like in the future, but I began to have an idea last year when my middle school required each student to participate in an extracurricular activity. I began my search for the one that was right for me, and finally I found Students Run L.A., a team that trains together to run the L.A. Marathon. This group was all about determination, not competition, and I was convinced that I was meant for it.

At my first practice, I felt like I was in a hospital waiting room as I waited and waited for the chance to start running—and eventually I did get to run instead of parking my bottom in a chair. We were asked to complete three laps around the park. As I ran alone, I saw other little groups of friends running together. I wanted to say hello but was too shy to do so. After I'd wanted so badly for the practice session to start, now I just wanted to go home and rest—now I couldn't wait for the practice to end. Although I was desperate to quit the group because I felt lonely, I knew it would be a mistake. I knew that on the following March 6, I would run the L.A. Marathon, alone if I had to.

One sunny day a week later, the entire team walked to a park to run a few practice laps. I was walking by myself when suddenly I felt the breath and heard the steps of someone behind me. I turned around and was surprised to see a smiling, orange-haired girl.

"Hi! What's your name?" she asked.

"Madeline. How 'bout yours?" I managed to speak despite my shock.

"Mireya," she answered.

We ran laps together that day and discovered that we ran at the same pace. After that, I looked forward to our practices. I also saw Mireya at school. I wanted to hang out with her, but she had her own group of friends who didn't seem to like me much.

Once when I was tagging along with Mireya and her friends Julie and Martha, I noticed Julie giving me nasty looks. I felt awful, unwanted and out of place. While I felt that it might be impossible to ever hang out with Mireya without having this wall between us, that wall didn't stop us from getting to know each other at practice. Like me, she liked to skateboard, run, and get good grades, and she often thought the same way I did.

"You know, you are so much like me," Mireya would tell me.

"You're right. We are like . . . sisters," I said.

"Yin and yang."

"Mireya and Madeline."

"M and M," we both said, cracking up. When we talked, we often would say the same thing at the same time, like we had planned it.

Mireya and I decided that we were each like the sisters we wished we had. I had a sister, but all she wanted to do was play with Barbies. Eventually, Mireya decided she wanted to hang out with me at school during lunch, and she gave up her old friends. Maybe I'd won that battle. We went everywhere together, just like sisters, with total trust and honesty between us.

We ran our races together, and the training period went by very quickly: first a one-mile race, then the three-, nine-, thirteen-, and the eighteen-mile runs. Next was the marathon! Mireya and I were both nervous about the race, and we talked on the phone every night, asking each other questions we couldn't answer.

"Are there going to be enough water stands?"

"What if it's canceled?"

"Is it true that your knees pop?"

Despite our fears, we knew that our training had prepared us well, and we were both determined to cross the finish line.

All of us in Students Run L.A. were full of excitement when our trainers informed us that the Telemundo television station wanted to interview us about running the marathon. Wow—we were going to be on TV!

On the day of the interview, we had to wake up at 2 AM and be ready by 4 AM, but I was so keyed up that I jumped out of bed as soon as my alarm clock sounded. Mireya and I and the rest of the team were taken to the Los Angeles Convention Center, where we found cameras and all kinds of equipment I had never seen before. The cameras were turned on, and we were on the air—and I was interviewed! The reporter asked me so many questions, and I was so excited that I could hardly remember what he asked or what I answered. Mireya's mom recorded the interview, and my family and I watched the video together later that day.

"You look fatter on TV," my mother pointed out.

I realized she was right. "How do models still look so thin?" I asked.

"I don't know, but I do know that I'm really proud of you." She hugged me really tight and gave me a kiss.

The night before the marathon, my stomach had butterflies that wouldn't fly away. I lay in bed and wondered about what things would be like the next morning. Many questions popped into my mind, including: What if I can't finish? What if I fall down and hurt myself? What if I don't wake up early enough and I get left behind? My imagination had gone out of control.

Suddenly, it was Sunday—it's mind-boggling how you go to sleep at night, and before you know it, it's morning. I quickly dressed in my marathon uniform, a tank top and some short shorts. My dad drove me to school, where a bus waited to take the team to the marathon. My nerves were going berserk, and I was ready to bite my nails off. I found Mireya on the bus, and we sat together, united in our anxiety.

The bus took us to a hotel in downtown L.A., and we got out and nervously stretched until it was time to move to the starting line. It was total chaos, with thousands of people milling around like busy animals. There were many supporters cheering us on, and many, many runners stretching and jogging over to the starting line. The faces of the young runners around us told us they were as nervous as we were.

Mireya and I made a plan. "We must run at least to mile five without stopping," she told me with a serious expression on her face.

"It'll be tough, but we should definitely try," I gulped.

We had no idea where the starting line was, so we just followed the crowd and waited for the race to start. Once we heard the starting pistol, we were off! I was running next to Mireya, but suddenly I lost sight of her. Where was she? I looked around desperately. Had I left her behind or had she sped off ahead?

Although I had to fulfill our promise, right then I only wanted to find Mireya. At last I spotted her, and soon we were running side by side, step by step. At each mile there was a sign showing how many miles we had run, and we both cheered at each sign and yelled out how many more we had ahead of us; at times we would have to use our fingers to do the subtracting.

Miles and miles went by. At mile fourteen we still hadn't had to walk, but then my dear friend began to get a side stitch (we called it "the bean"). "I can't run much more," she told me, taking big breaths. "I need to stop and walk a little." While I really wanted to stay with her, I'd come this far, and I wanted to keep the fastest pace I could for as long as possible. I was forced to leave her behind, but Mireya didn't mind.

A little farther along the route, I saw my parents standing on the sidewalk, cheering and supporting me, and this made me want to cry. I ran on, and I kept running, and then I too began to get "the bean." I had a battle now, a battle against myself: I was sore, sweaty, and worn out. My weakness told me to stop running, so I began to walk. But then a voice inside me, my inner strength, told me to go on. So I ran some more.

At around mile twenty-four, all of the runners were going so slowly they looked liked old grandparents using walkers. Suddenly, I heard Mireya yelling behind me. She caught up with me, her face red and sweaty, but soon she began to walk again. I told her I was going to run the rest of the way, and she encouraged me and told me she'd see me at the finish line. So I ran and ran and finally saw the finish line—I did it, I told myself. I did it! I had won the battle, broken through that wall, and finished the marathon. As I crossed the line, a tear rolled down my cheek. I waited for Mireya until she too crossed the finish line, crying and filled with excitement.

"We finished!" we told each other as we hugged.

Running the marathon was the greatest L.A. experience I've ever had. It is an unforgettable memory. I'm now training for this year's marathon. Mireya is my best friend, and we've told each other we will run marathons together until we are seventy or older. We've invited other friends to run with us, and they have accepted.

I was just looking for an extracurricular activity, but I found much more than I expected—I found a talent I can be proud of, and I made a friend for life. Marathon buddies. Sisters. M and M. Mireya and Madeline.

HALF-INDIAN, BUT FULL LATINA
MINERVA HENRIQUEZ

My mom stands in front of the stove, making enchiladas with lots of cheese, just they way I like them. She is a short little woman, but loud. I can hear her from the corner when she screams my name. I'm only in my bedroom, a room away from the kitchen, but she yells as if I'm miles away.

"Mini, *venme a ayudar,*" my mom calls to me.

I slowly walk to the kitchen and watch her cook. She flips one tortilla in the *comal,* she has another tortilla in the pan with the red chili sauce, and she's folding one more with cheese. It's ready to eat, so she puts it on the plate.

I stand there, watching her. Then I go get a cup of water and sit on the chair by the front of the stove. She just wants me to be there with her. "You're done talking on the phone?" she asks in Spanish. That's her language. She was born in El Salvador.

I respond with a "*si.*"

My mom: light skin, short, big hips, small pointy nose. Me: brown skin, taller than my mom, longer nose, and big eyes.

As she makes the enchiladas, I observe that the only thing that makes us the same is our wavy hair and the dimple in our chins. My mom looks like a Latina woman; as for me, I look like a young Indian woman. My father was born in India—I never met him, but I inherited his looks. Although I'm half-Indian in blood, I'm full Latina in culture. I would be so happy if I were simply Latina, like my nine-year-old sister: she is Salvadoran like my mother, and Mexican, like her father, the man who raised me. I really don't know what to call myself when people ask me what I am, so I say "Salvadoran, Mexican, and Indian." I'm always confused about my identity.

When people see us in the streets, they never think my mom is my mother because she looks like a Latina and I look Indian. We may not look alike, but she's like my best friend. My mom was single until I was six, and she worked really hard to give me all the things that children with both parents would have. She is 4'11", serious, and always mad because my sister and I don't clean our rooms, but she is a good woman, someone I can talk to about my problems and who always gives me good advice. We go shopping almost every Saturday; we try on a lot of clothes but just buy one thing. We laugh a lot and don't like people to tell us what to do. And we both hate to be wrong. But she is overprotective and jealous, and I'm worried about how she will react to my relationship with a boy. It hasn't happened—yet!

While my mom and I are in the kitchen, I can hear my stepfather hammering out in the garden. He is 5'7", a dark-skinned man, and a generous and kind person. And he's really funny. Sometimes when I tell him, "Dad, you were asleep," he says, "No, my eyes were just closed," although he was snoring. When I talk to him he always tries to change the meaning of what I say, like when I say "my school," he says, "When did you buy the school?" Or sometimes when I use the phrase "the whole world," he says "Do you know the whole world?" I get mad because I'm trying to make a point, and he pretends that he doesn't understand, even though I know he does. Sometimes he does listen, like when my mom calls his name: "Francisco, *ven para ca.*" He goes with no questions. He always listens to her.

My mom met my stepdad when I was five. He used to have an auto shop at the corner of 4th Street and Lorena, and my mom and I lived in the apartments next door. I was six when they got married. At first I was jealous: I just wanted my mom for myself and didn't want to share her with anyone; I used to tell her that I would kill myself if she dated him. When he sat down at the dinner table, I refused to eat. But he won me over, eventually, by taking me to movies and out for pizza. My feelings changed, and I started realizing that Don Francisco was a good man, and I learned to love him as my father. Sometimes I wish I were his real daughter so I could say that I'm Mexican and Salvadoran. It seems like an easier identity to explain, and one I would like claim.

Time has gone so fast. I'm now seventeen. As my mother finishes folding the tortillas with the cheese inside, I think of something else: a guy that I like, the guy I just got off the phone with. He has asked me to be his girlfriend, and I have no idea how I'm going to talk to my mom about it. I don't know how to start—I feel happy that he asked me out, but also bad because I know that my mom is not going to like the idea of her child wanting to have a boyfriend.

"Minerva, *despierta ya vamos a comer.*"

My mom has finished making the enchiladas. She puts our plates on the table and sits down with me.

I'm nervous, and I can't look her in the eyes because I feel ashamed. "What's wrong, why don't you eat?" she asks me. I have to tell her. I know it's the perfect time because it is just her and me. She asks again, "Come on, what's the matter?"

I say, "Mom, I need to tell you something."

"*Que?*"

"Mom, you know the guy I was talking on the phone with? Well, he asked me if I wanted to be his girlfriend," I explain. "I said yes, but I want your permission, Mom."

She stares at me with a sad face. I'm disappointed by her reaction, but not surprised. She says, "I need to meet him. And I need to talk to your great-aunts about this. I need advice." Although they are great-aunts, I call them my aunts.

My aunts are good women who were there for me when I was small. I love them and I see them as my second moms, and when I hear that my mom plans to ask their advice, I feel hopeful.

The next day we go to my Aunt Graciela's, a clean elegant home. My three aunts are there. I don't want to look them in the eyes. I feel like I have somehow done something wrong, although I know there's nothing wrong with wanting to date.

My aunt Graciela lies on the floor. She is a slim, tall woman with black curly hair who is always thinking about her physical appearance and the calories she eats. But she is also the coolest, the one who gets on roller coasters with me and does other crazy stuff. And she understands me, especially when it comes to boys, because when she was a teenager she had a lot of boyfriends.

My aunt Olga sits on the couch. She loves food and doesn't care about the calories; she is always complaining about her weight but doesn't do anything about it. She is always loud and exaggerated in her ideas. She is also the one who spoils me and does anything to make me happy, including lying to my mother in my defense. She is the one who constantly hugs me and makes me feel like a baby.

My aunt Daniela sits on a chair. Always wearing a sweater, she looks quite serious with her glasses and her hair in a loose bun. She is quiet and almost never talks, only when she really has something to say. She is also really calm and mature—she thinks before doing something. She is wise and always gives good advice.

My mom sits down on the couch next to Aunt Olga. She looks

confident that she will win my aunts to her side and that they will all say "no" to a boyfriend for me. She sits there with her chin up.

All these women are part of me: looking at them is like looking at four versions of myself. I have a loud laugh like my mom, and like her, I am happy all the time. I try to take care of my shape and I worry about the things I eat, like my Aunt Graciela. Like my Aunt Olga, I am affectionate and sensitive, wanting to make others happy. Like my Aunt Daniela, I think before doing something.

I can't bear to stay in the room, so I walk into the kitchen where I can still hear everything they say.

"*Esta muchacha quiere tener novio,*" I hear my mom say. This girl wants to have a boyfriend.

My Aunt Olga says, "But she is so small, with a frightened face."

My Aunt Graciela says, still lying down with her eyes closed, "Well, at that age I already had a lot of boyfriends, and Minerva is already seventeen."

My Aunt Daniela, with her hands in her lap, says, "Alma, let her have a boyfriend; she's mature enough to handle it."

And my Aunt Olga says, "But her schoolwork. Will she be distracted?"

My mom says, in a loud voice that she intends for me to hear, "If Minerva lowers her grades, I'm going to break up that relationship!"

My Aunt Graciela says, "She says he's an usher at his church—that's a good thing."

"But they can't go out by themselves!" exclaims Aunt Olga, who is obviously remembering her own dating days.

My mom says loudly, "Her sister will have to go out with them." She approves! At least, I think she does. Then she finishes: ". . . if I decide to let them go out." Shoot, I'm back where I started.

My Aunt Daniela says, "Well, my daughter had her boyfriend when she was fifteen and nothing bad happened."

My aunt Graciela gets up and sits next to my mom. "Look, Alma, the boy looks like a nice guy, and if you don't give her permission she is still going to see him. It's better if you give them permission—then you are in control."

"I'm still not sure," my mom says.

"Keep this in mind: having a boyfriend doesn't mean she is going to marry him," my Aunt Graciela says.

Sitting in the kitchen, I think that it's two against two: my Aunt Olga and my Mom against Graciela and Daniela. I'm still so nervous, but now I'm feeling hopeful.

I am still in the kitchen when my mom calls my name. "Minerva, *ven!*"

I go in the living room with my head down. And she tells me, "It is OK, you can have a boyfriend. But you are only going to see him on Friday, Saturday, and Sunday, and that is only if you have no homework."

I smile and quietly say, "Thank you!" I can't wait to get on the phone and give him the news. It's over!

My mom still looks serious. As I look at her, I remember when I was small: I didn't want my mom to have a boyfriend, either. I was jealous because I thought that she was going to forget about me, but she didn't. Thinking about that, I understand how my Mom feels now, and I understand why she's been so upset.

I realize that even though my mom and I may not look alike, we have the same interiors. We share the same values and culture, and we are more similar than different, no matter how society may see our skins. And I realize that the people who give me their love and who are there with me every day, advising me in the decisions I make—my mom, my aunts, my stepdad—are what form my identity, not my blood, my appearance, or my ethnicity.

OPPOSITES ATTRACT
ANA RIOS

It is September 6, 2003. My friends and I have made plans to go to Universal CityWalk and watch a new movie that opens tonight. We are known as "the film freaks" because we never miss any movie premieres. I've just finished getting ready and am on the phone with Janet.

"Hey Janet, are you ready?" I ask.

"Hey Sarah, almost. All the girls are here so you can pick us up at my house."

When I get to Janet's house, all the film freaks are waiting for me.

"Hey," they say with excitement as they get into the car.

"Are you ready to see the new movie? It's supposed to be the best movie of the year," I say.

We arrive at CityWalk. It is so crowded, and we pass so many different people on our way to the movie theater to buy our tickets. We want to get a bite to eat first at the food court, and we decide to go to Tommy's Burgers. As we sit at a table, out of nowhere, some guys approach us.

"Are you ladies here with anyone?" one of the guys asks.

"No," Janet replies in an instant.

"May we join you?"

We pause for a moment and look at one another and decide it's fine for them to join us.

"Please excuse my friend," says the tall, cute one with a nice smile. "It seems my friend has no manners. My name is Charlie and this is Gregory."

"My name is Sarah," I say. "And this is Janet and Stephanie and Michelle."

"Nice to meet you," he says.

They join us at the table and then for the movie. Just before the movie starts, Charlie asks, "Can I sit next to you?"

"Yes," I reply.

I'm so excited. I can't believe Charlie asked if he can sit next to me. Charlie puts his arm around me, and I'm so happy, because never in my life has a guy, let alone a cute guy, put his arm around me.

After the movie is over, Charlie asks, "Would you like a ride home?" I realize that I drove here—and I really wish I hadn't.

"I would, but I drove," I say.

"Don't worry about that; I'll drive your car home," Janet says.

"Are you sure?"

"Yes, don't worry."

"You're the best."

Charlie and I head to his car. "So where do you live, Sarah?" he asks.

"I live in East L.A. Where do you live?" I ask him.

"Beverly Hills."

"It must be nice to live in Beverly Hills."

"Yeah, but some people think that I'm some kind of stuck-up, spoiled brat, when really I'm not. People shouldn't judge someone by where they live."

When we get to my house, Charlie says, "Good night, Sarah. Can I have your phone number?"

Of course, I gave it to him.

At home, I put on my pajamas. I am in my bed hoping and waiting for his phone call, when all of a sudden my cell phone rings.

"Hi, Sarah, what are you doing?" Charlie says.

"Just getting ready for tomorrow," I reply.

"I just called to say good night and sweet dreams," he says.

I can't believe that Charlie called just to say good night and sweet dreams! Even though I am tired after such a long day, I still manage to have a big smile on my face.

✖

"Wake up, young lady, time to go to school," my mother says.

I wake up with the same smile that I went to sleep with, and for some reason, I can't stop thinking about Charlie. I can't wait to get to school and tell all my friends about him.

"Hey Sarah, how was your ride home?" Janet asks.

"It was the best night of my life, Janet. He took me straight home, and he was such a gentleman. After he dropped me off, he called right after I finished putting my pajamas on, and it was the sweetest thing ever. He said he was just calling to wish me sweet dreams," I say.

"Oh my goodness, I'm so totally jealous. What else?"

"Nothing—I'm just waiting for him call again."

48

✻

After school, and to my surprise, Charlie is waiting for me outside the school's front gate. He is wearing a leather jacket and holding two helmets, and he is standing next to a motorcycle.

"Hey, Charlie, what are you doing here? This is such a nice surprise," I say.

"I couldn't wait to see you, so I decided to drop by. Do you want to go have a bite to eat?"

"Sure—there's this great taco stand on the way to my house," I suggest.

We ride to the taco stand on Charlie's motorcycle and order some tacos, and as we eat them, we speak about our lives and dreams.

"So, Sarah, what do you want to do when you grow up?"

"I've always wanted to be a kindergarten teacher in East L.A., working with little kids, helping them learn their ABCs and how to tie their shoes," I answer.

He says, "I really like the fact that you have goals and things you are looking forward to, because to tell you the truth, nowadays it is really hard to find someone with goals and dreams."

"Yeah, I know; if it weren't for my parents always being there, pushing me to work harder, I don't think that I would be as focused on my future as I am now. What are your goals in life?"

"Well, right now I'm playing football at USC, but I'm really looking forward to playing professional football. Like your parents, my parents have always had a big influence on my future."

"Charlie, it's getting a little late; I think we should get going."

Charlie agrees, so we get back on his motorcycle and head home.

When we arrive at my house, Charlie again asks, "Can I call you later?" And of course, again I say yes.

My mother is waiting for me just inside the door. "Where have you been, young lady?" she asks once I'm inside the house.

"I was out with a friend."

"What friend?"

"Charlie," I say.

✻

I am in my room trying to do my homework, but I can hardly concentrate because I can't stop thinking about Charlie and how cute he looked on his motorcycle, and how beautiful his eyes were when the sun shone in them. My phone rings, awakening me—I had fallen asleep while doing my homework.

"Hey Sarah, can you talk?" Charlie says.

"No, I'm doing my homework," I reply, so he says he will call later.

After I finish my homework, I start setting the table for dinner.

"Sarah, the guy that brought you home today—was that Charlie?" my mother asks.

"Yes," I reply.

"I think that we should meet your new friend; you should invite him for dinner so your father and I can get to know him," my mother says. I tell her I'll ask him.

Later, I am in my bedroom reading a book called *The Perks of Being a Wallflower;* it's the best book I've read so far this year. I meditate on whether I really want Charlie to come and have dinner at my house or not—I'm getting the feeling that he might not like my house or think I'm not good enough for him. Finally, I find the courage to call him.

"Hello, Charlie. I hope you're not busy. Listen, I was wondering if you wanted to come over for dinner tomorrow night."

"Yes, I would love to," Charlie says.

"Great. Then I'll see you tomorrow at seven."

"Seven it is."

"I should let you go; it's getting late."

"Good night and sweet dreams."

"Good night."

※

Today is the day my parents will meet Charlie. It is now seven o'clock, and he is on time. He is already making a good impression.

"Nice to meet you, Mr. and Mrs. Lopez. I'm Charlie."

"Nice to meet you, Charlie," my parents say.

My mom has prepared her special dish, *arroz con gandules* (Puerto Rican rice). My parents want to know all about this new boy from Beverly Hills.

"So Charlie, I hear you play football at USC. What position?" my father asks.

"I'm the quarterback, sir."

After more polite conversation about school and football, it is time for

Charlie to leave. But before he leaves, he stops before the door, looking a bit nervous.

"Before I leave, Mr. and Mrs. Lopez, I would like to ask Sarah if she wants to be my girlfriend—if that's OK with you?" Charlie asks.

"Yes, it's OK," my father replies.

Then, as I look at him with a big smile, I say, "Absolutely."

Charlie leaves, and I think my parents are impressed with him. My father really loves the fact that he plays football at USC. I call Charlie to say good night, because the faster I go to sleep, the faster tomorrow will come.

�֍

A few weeks later, feeling that Charlie and I are getting much closer, I invite him to attend church with my family. After church Charlie and I decide to get something to eat. We are sitting in a restaurant when, out of nowhere, Charlie says something very surprising.

"Sarah, I just want you to know that you are very special and you mean the whole world to me—I love you."

"I love you too, Charlie," I say.

"I was wondering if you would like to meet my parents, because I want them to meet the love of my life," he says.

I reply, "Yes, I would love to."

Charlie takes me home, and at my front door, he says, "Good-bye. I'll pick you up tomorrow at 6:30 . . . and I love you." And then kisses me.

All afternoon I think about Charlie's parents, if they will like me, and what I will wear to dinner.

✗

Tonight I will meet Charlie's parents. I can't wait, I am so excited to finally meet them.

Charlie picks me up, and on the way to his house, I ask, "Charlie, what if they don't like me? What if they end up hating me? What if I make a fool of myself in front of them?"

"Don't worry about it. They're going to love you," he says. We are in Charlie's neighborhood now, and you can really see a difference between East L.A. and Beverly Hills. It's so clean, and you see about three Mercedes in front of each house. Charlie's house is enormous compared to mine: it's a

two-story home with a front lawn as big as our whole house. I am so nervous about meeting Charlie's parents, who are waiting for us at the door.

"Mom, Dad—this is Sarah," Charlie says. "Sarah, these are my parents."

"Nice to meet you, Mr. and Mrs. Hughes."

"Very nice to meet you, Sarah," they say.

We have a very nice meal followed by apple pie for dessert. Charlie's
parents begin to ask me questions about myself.

"So, Sarah, where do you live?"

"East L.A.," I reply.

"Oh, is that so." And they ask me about my parents and what they
do. As soon as they find out I live in East L.A., their whole attitude
changes—they ignore me as if I weren't in the same room with them. At
this point, I have millions of worried thoughts going through my head.

When it's time for me to go, I don't think his parents are as impressed
with me as my parents were with him. We get into Charlie's car and head
back to my house.

"So, did you like my parents?" Charlie asks me.

"Yeah, I liked *them,* but I'm not so sure they liked *me.*"

"Of course they liked you."

"No, they didn't, Charlie. They didn't like that I live in East L.A."

"My parents are not like that," he says. I didn't say anything else.

We arrive at my house and I turn to get out of the car.

"Good night, Sarah. I had a nice time."

"Same here, Charlie," I say, even though I feel horrible.

Charlie kisses me good-bye, but we can both feel that things are
not right.

I go to my room, put on my pajamas, and start reading my book.
Then I start feeling melancholy when I remember how Charlie's parents'
whole attitude towards me changed just because I live in East L.A. At last
Charlie calls.

"Hey Sarah, my love," Charlie says.

"Hey," I answer quietly.

"Why do you sound so sad?"

"I just feel bad about your parents not liking me."

"Don't worry about that. As long as I love you, that's all that really
matters."

"So you agree that they don't like me, Charlie?" I ask.

"It's just that they don't like me dating you," he answers.

"What do you mean?"

"Sarah, they threatened me—they told me that I have to break up with you in order to be able to play football."

"No! Charlie, please tell me that this is a joke."

"No, Sarah, it's not a joke, but no matter what, I am never going to leave you, even if it means that I have to stop playing football."

"Charlie, I won't let you do that—it's your dream to become a professional football player. Please let me have tonight to think about it."

"What do you mean, 'think about it'? There's nothing to think about."

"Please, Charlie. I'll get back to you in the morning."

"OK. I love you so much."

"I love you too, Charlie."

"Good night," he says sweetly.

"Good night," I reply, barely able to control my tears.

I lie in my bed, crying my eyes out, wanting to scream but not being able to. I am thinking about Charlie, about how much I would miss him if I had to break up with him. But despite how I feel, I am going to break up with him anyway, because it is better for his future—not to mention better for mine, since I don't think that Charlie's parents would ever accept the fact that I'm from East L.A.

✖

The next morning, even though I don't want to, I call Charlie.

"Hey," I say.

"Hey," he replies. waiting for what I'm going to say.

"Charlie, you know that I love you with all of my heart and that you mean the whole world to me. But I think it's better for us to take a break and let your parents cool down for a little while."

"No, Sarah, I love you," he pleads.

"Please don't make this any harder than it already is. I love you and you will always have a special place in my heart. Good-bye, Charlie." And I hang up the phone before I start to cry—again.

A NURSE'S LIFE
KEREN HERNANDEZ

I used to think that what a pediatric nurse did for her community was feed and change babies while mothers rested after giving birth. Because I have always loved babies and enjoy taking care of them, I thought that being a pediatric nurse would be a perfect career for me. I would care for newborns; I would walk into hospital waiting rooms and show healthy babies to happy families.

And then I learned that there is much more to pediatric nursing.

Nothing bad had ever happened to my family until two years ago, and when something tragic did happen, I realized how valuable the job of a pediatric nurse truly is.

I went with my cousin Mary, who was eight-and-a-half months pregnant, to her standard prenatal checkup. Not wanting to go alone, she invited me to accompany her because her husband Mike was at work. Looking at Mary, I could see how happy she was that soon she would have her baby in her arms, giving it her love.

While the doctor was examining her, I looked at his face. He looked worried. He told Mary that he wanted to keep her in the hospital because she was soon going to be in labor. I could tell that something was wrong, but I didn't ask what it was; I was afraid that if it was really bad news, I would become emotional and not be able to support Mary.

I waited with Mary for twenty minutes until Mike arrived. When he came into the room, his face was red and his eyes were watery, and I got nervous. He came over to me and said "Hey," like he always did, and then he took my hand and gave me a kiss on the cheek.

"Would you mind waiting outside? I have something important to talk to Mary about," he said sadly.

Mike did not want to tell me what was happening because he knew I was going to start crying, and he was not going to be able to comfort me. I walked out of the room and sat alone in the waiting area. Ten minutes later, my entire family arrived. My older sister was crying, and my mom and my little sister both had watery eyes. What really caught my attention was my father; it was the first time I had ever seen him cry, and it scared me; he never cried in front of us.

Apparently I was the only one who didn't know what was happening. My mom came over to me and asked, "Has anyone told you what is going on?"

"No," I said. "Please tell me."

Then she hugged me and told me that the baby had died. He had gotten tangled with the umbilical cord and had choked. Now I understood why everyone was so sad.

I looked at my mom and started crying uncontrollably. I could not believe what was happening. We were all so excited about the baby: I had looked forward to talking to him, I had felt his kick. I was in love with him before he was even born, and now he was gone. I could only imagine how Mike and Mary were feeling.

When I went into the room where Mike and Mary were, they were looking at their baby. He was a beautiful baby—so small and cute. But when I touched him, he was so cold. It was hard to watch Mike touch the baby because he would start crying; Mary was not crying because they had given her a sedative. The nurse walked over to the bed and gave Mary the baby, wrapped in a blanket, so she could hold him.

"I'm sorry for your loss," she said, and then she turned and hugged Mike with compassion.

It was then that I realized that a nurse is not just someone who takes care of healthy babies—a nurse is there during times of both joy and sadness. What happened to my cousin was horrible, and even though the nurse wanted to do something to make the grieving parents feel better, she could not. She could not bring the baby back to life. Even though a compassionate nurse suffers the loss with her patients, she is there to offer support to grieving families—that's why nurses are so important.

You might think that this sad experience made me change my mind about becoming a nurse in my community, but it did not—the experience made me stronger and more determined to pursue my dream of becoming a pediatric nurse in Los Angeles.

EAST L.A.: MY 'HOOD, MY HOME, MY HEART
WENDY RODRIGUEZ

"For I know the plans I have for you," declares the Lord. "Plans to prosper you and not to harm you, plans to give you hope, and a future" (Jeremiah 29:11).

I was raised in East in L.A.—yes, East L.A. When people think of my neighborhood, they think of the ghetto, drugs, police pursuits, gangs, drive-bys, and cruel, coldhearted murderers. But I have to object: East L.A. is where I have grown to be the strong, intelligent, and savvy person that I am today. East L.A. is where I have lived my life, where I've found friends, lost friends, where I've attended elementary, middle, and high school. It's also where I've found love, been accepted, and most of all, where I have experienced good and bad situations—but mostly good. The truth is, my East L.A. is not what you see on television or in movies. I want to share with you the reality of *my* East L.A.

My mom and my two sisters and brother and I lived all over the neighborhood before settling into a beige stucco apartment building at Lorena and Atlantic streets. There are two rows of apartments like mine, facing each other. As soon as I walk outside I see a twenty-five-foot-high concrete wall that is "autographed" every day by graffiti "artists" in the neighborhood; it gets painted over almost every other day. On the other side of that wall is a busy freeway where trailers rumble by at 5 AM—it's my alarm clock to wake me up for school. However, if I look to the right I see the bright, vibrant reds, blues, and yellows of the Lorena Street Elementary School mural. It's a beautiful painting of the alphabet, with each letter illustrating a different career: for example, the letter *f* stands for "firefighter," and the words "firefighter" and the Spanish word for firefighter, "*bombero*," are painted in bright colors.

The true character of a neighborhood is not always obvious at first glance. My neighborhood is about hanging out with friends, having get-togethers with neighbors, and making plenty of noise—but happy noise, the noise of voices laughing and of people helping each other.

There are four older women in my apartment complex named Maria.

The Maria who lives across from my apartment not only takes care of her lush, eye-catching garden filled with roses, green plants, and *guayaba* and avocado trees, but she also takes the time to rake the leaves in our yard. My sister and I used to cut the dusty red roses from another Maria's garden for my mother. One day we got caught, and Maria promised to buy us our own rosebush for our own rose garden, but she never did; nearly ten years later, my sister still jokes about waiting for her rosebush. When I think about my neighborhood, I see all these little things that make it special, the details that make my surroundings beautiful.

Food is very important to the people of our neighborhood. On cold rainy afternoons, my sister Lucia and I walk home from school together. We smell the aromas of traditional Mexican dishes drifting out into the street from every kitchen on the block. Women of the neighborhood prepare *caldo de pollo* (chicken soup), *champurrado* (a thick, sweet drink), and my mom's specialty, *pozole*. *Pozole* is a blend of pork and hominy served with diced onion, sliced radish, cilantro, and a squeeze of lemon. It's spicy, not so spicy that you have to drink a whole gallon of water to put out the flames, but enough that it's rich in flavor. And of course, *tostadas*—can't leave those out.

In the movies you see hard-core, bald-headed *cholos* in school with bandanas, hairnets, flannel shirts, and size-40 501s. My high school is not like that; we have a dress code, so none of that stuff is allowed. There are people I know who don't care about changing for a better future. They say, "Oh no, I don't want to change," or "Oh no, people won't accept me." Everyone is destined to a great future. If you really want something, you have to go and get it, not just talk about it. I say, "Be the doer, not the talker."

I try my best to get what I want, with help from others or by myself. The Humanitas Academy here at Roosevelt High School has prepared me to look into my future: I plan to go to college and get my degree in early childhood education. My dream is to teach kindergarten-aged children at Lorena Street Elementary School where I once learned.

One of the most rewarding and challenging experiences I'vd had at Roosevelt High School has been my involvement with the *folklórico* dance tradition. *Folklórico* is a style of Mexican dance performed to a variety of musical styles, including *mariachi, huasteco, banda,* and *norteño.* The girls wear long, beautiful dresses with multicolored ribbons and bright flowers in their hair; the boys wear jackets, boots, and scarves. The costumes vary depending on the region where a particular dance comes from. In the five years that I have danced *folklórico*, we've performed all over Los Angeles, at retirement homes, hospitals, Downtown's Placita Olvera, even Disneyland. Learning different regional dances, performing them for people and seeing their happy faces, I realize that I am a part of a younger generation that is keeping the rich Mexican tradition alive. Learning to dance *folklórico* has taught me to be patient, to be committed, and to never give up.

No matter where I go, I know I'm always going to be brought back to East L.A. by my memories. East L.A. will never leave me—it's like a permanent scar. All of my memories are from here; my family, my teachers, my friends are all here. I may not live in East L.A. my whole life, but I will never be far away, either physically or in spirit.

AN ODD DAY
DIMAS ORTIZ

My friends and I are playing soccer on our field
Near our orange-colored homes with many trees around
We are very competitive with each other
That is what makes it more fun
It is slanted, muddy, and grassy
On one side we mark the goal with trash
On the other we use trees and soccer balls
Many are dressed like *cholos*
With baggy shorts and long shirts
In black, blue, and white
Many think that we are *cholos* wearing these colors
But most of us are not
At the bottom of the field
Four cop cars stop
I see them running toward us
It is confusing
They start yelling insulting names at us
"Beaners"
"Wetbacks"
We were just playing soccer.

One of my friends starts running
We all get scared and run with him
Each of us runs in a different direction and hides
One of my friends keeps running
And gets tackled in the McDonald's parking lot
With his body on the ground
They keep on yelling at him
"Stay down!"
"Don't struggle!"
I close my eyes

When I open them I see him getting released
The police thought
He was someone else.
They had the wrong kid.
And we were just playing soccer.

LIKE A RACE
EDWIN CERVANTES (E.T.)

I stand alone, watching, waiting, dreaming
I dream of L.A. and what I want to be
My friends passing away, I really hate to see
Petey in the ground
'Cause his skin was brown
As I hope to live another day
Wishing it didn't have to be this way
L.A. is my city, my place
Living here is like a race
Racing to stay alive
Racing to never die
Maylo lost the race
He was at the wrong place
Shopping for his daughter
Now the girl has no father
As I'm wanting to succeed
To never ever live in greed
I hear a shot from a gun
They think I shot it so I start to run
I see people bleed
Like me, they're from the same seed
Police chase others
As I hear their crying mothers

I stand alone, watching, waiting, dreaming
To live and die in L.A.
That's what I love to say
L.A. is my home

LOS ANGELES THROUGH MY EYES
HECTOR RODRIGUEZ

I see many crying and suffering
Mothers weeping over dead sons and daughters
Fathers drinking their life away
Beating their family when they have a bad day
Social workers stepping in, placing the children into foster care
Children never seeing their families again

I see teens getting caught up in the gang life because they feel like
they have to be bad
Many paranoid about getting smoked when they're not looking
Making their families suffer and worry every time they don't come
home for weeks
I see them put six feet under and their families crying because they
lost a son or daughter or cousin . . .

I see a drug problem that has been on the rise for many years
Making many people crave every other minute trying to get fixed
Stealing from their own mothers and little brothers trying to get
fixed for the hour
Many doing whatever it takes to get their hands on the medicine
that they need

I see parents working hard but never making enough money
Working long hours but getting paid minimum wage
Working hard for their families to get by each day
Crying every time their kid asks them for something that they saw
on the television
Knowing that they don't have money to get them what they want

I see little kids that just don't care about life anymore
Wondering why they should work like their parents and get nothing

As opposed to selling drugs and getting it all
Not knowing the dangers they put on themselves and others
Thinking that life can be easy if they make the quick money

I see families here for a better future, but their children wanting
the worst
Thinking that they can turn to the streets for a living
They don't want to work for their money
Wanting to hurt those who hurt them
They want it all, but they don't know what it means or takes
I see people dying every night
I see the shootings on the block
I see murderers creep up on a car and shoot like there is no
tomorrow
Everyone sees this, but what do they do? Nothing much
They put more police in the area, but it's not enough
They harass us when they see us
They are here "to protect and to serve," but how will they protect
us if they can't protect themselves
They think that we don't know that we outnumber the police,
but when the revolution comes who will they protect?

I see beauty in this demanding city, beauty in parks and schools
and families
Full of culture and activities
But many don't see what's on the other side of this fairy-tale life
that people claim to be living

THE BATTLE
JACKELINE MARTINEZ

I live in East Los Angeles in the projects. For some the projects are the ghetto, for others the projects are a refuge, and for still others the projects are a hole of ignorance that eats everyone alive—every day it devours. To live in the projects is a daily battle between excellent and dreadful. Some people give up and stop fighting, others never surrender. But everything negative has something positive.

Once I step off my porch, the battle begins. The gang members appear when you least expect them. The nasty smell of drugs fills the atmosphere. As I set out to school in the morning, I see other kids who are also going to school, and deep inside my heart I know that there is hope.

As I walk home from school and approach the projects, everything is quiet. I pass by some corners and the gang members appear. Their eyes are gloomy; they look at me and they start scolding me. They call me "Rikishi!," because according to them I have a big behind! As I walk past them they blow me kisses and chase me home. I just ignore them and walk as fast as I can. As I walk to my apartment, I pass by the basketball courts; I hear the sound the ball makes when it is being dribbled. All of a sudden a rush of happiness comes over me. Memories come crushing down on me, and I feel safe, because basketball was once a part of my life, but as I walk by the basketball courts I encounter gang members playing basketball. I take a deep breath, and all of a sudden I don't feel safe anymore.

After I leave the basketball courts behind, I walk one more block, which seems to take an eternity. As I walk that block I feel that someone is chasing me! I walk as fast as the wind. Once I get to my apartment, I ring the doorbell; my sister opens the door for me. I step inside my apartment and I close the door behind me. I abscond from the dark world and enter another dimension.

My apartment is like a castle full of jewels. It is beautiful like a rose that is about to bloom. It is full of hope, happiness, and love. At home I do my homework, eat, and clean the house. As I perform my activities, the night takes over the day. As the night comes crawling down, more gang members come out. They stand on those dark corners like owls stand on a tree. I lie down on my bed and think about tomorrow.

Tomorrow will be a new day, and I prepare myself mentally to depart from home and continue the battle!

THE TURNS IN LIFE
EVELYN MARTINEZ

On my fourteenth birthday, Mama threw me a surprise party, the first one I'd ever had. To get me out of the house while Mama and my sister prepared for the party, Papa and I went for a walk to Oregon Park. After our little walk, we trekked up the big hill on Rowan Street to our house. As soon as I opened the door, twenty or so mouths yelled out, "Surprise!" Cheering along with Mama were various members of my family, aunts and uncles and some cousins whose names I didn't even remember. They were all there to celebrate my birthday. It was the first time I had ever had such a big party because it was the first time we had a house large enough to have one.

I greeted all twenty people (and relearned the names of those cousins), and as soon as I completed that last obligatory hug, we all went outside to the backyard to eat *carne asada*—not exactly my favorite food, but I gobbled it up anyway. While I sat at the round picnic table nibbling on my mediocre taco, I looked out toward Downtown and gazed at the buildings. I loved how they looked in the afternoon when the sun made them shiny.

Staring at the metal-and-glass skyscrapers had been my favorite pastime since we moved into this home nearly a month earlier. The perfect spot to stand to get the best view of them was right by the edge of the fence that divided our neighbor's property from ours. I could see everything from there—from Downtown Los Angeles to El Mercadito shopping center in East L.A.

It was finally time to open presents. The first one I picked up was from my older sister, Margarita; I anxiously wondered what it could be. My gut suggested it was probably one of those orange photo albums Margarita always gave me that I never used (and orange was my least favorite color). As I pried open the purple wrapping paper, making sure not to tear even a piece, I couldn't believe my eyes when I saw that it was a thin book of poetry by my favorite poet, Emily Dickinson. When she saw my elated expression she said, "I knew you'd like it," and knowingly added, "That's why we're sisters."

"I've never received such a great present!" I told her. We hugged for a couple of seconds—but not long enough.

When the last person left at four o'clock, I sat outside on our front porch. Being on the porch was strange for me, because before we moved here, we didn't have a porch; we lived in a building right in the center of Downtown off Pico Boulevard. I liked the new house a lot. It was small, mostly white, with beige doors and beige shutters around the windows, and an avocado tree grew in the front yard. The tree was so big that the roots came up all over the entire yard. There was also a *guayaba* tree, but no one liked to eat its fruit because it tasted too bland; Mama said that the fruit didn't taste good because it came from an old tree, but I liked how the *guayabas* smelled. I could smell them even from my bedroom window. The one thing I didn't like was that big hill I had to walk up to get home. But without that arduous walk up the hill, which I had nick-named Tiresome Hill, I wouldn't have such a great view of Downtown and beyond.

I sat on the porch reading my favorite book by Judy Blume, *Are You There God? It's Me, Margaret.* I knew I could finish it that night, but it meant sacrificing one hour of addictive TV. The book was worth it, though, even if I had to miss *The Simpsons*, my favorite show.

Inside the house, however, I heard Papa and Mama arguing about money once again. Mama complained that Papa wasn't bringing enough home. She yelled, "Why can't you ever keep a job?"

And then I heard Margarita say quietly, "It's not his fault he got laid off."

Then Papa shouted at Margarita, "This doesn't involve you! It's between me and your mother."

Margarita burst out the door, having been yelled at unreasonably one too many times. With not even a word to me, she jumped into her red Honda and drove off. She took a right onto Rowan, and I knew exactly where she was going.

Margarita had always been there for me, but as we got older I noticed that she had changed. When we were younger, she would always tie my shoelaces when they came untied, and we would play with Barbies for hours and hours. These days, however, Margarita wouldn't let me go any-where with her. She chose to spend all her time with her boyfriend and not me—he stole her from me.

Still, I knew her well enough to know where she was going: she called it *El lugar del olvido*—the place of forgetting. She took me there once, and I fell in love with it too.

When Margarita first discovered *El lugar del olvido,* she was taking the bus to an appointment with a new dentist. Somehow she got off at the wrong stop, and she frantically paced up and down the street looking at the building numbers. She asked a woman in a polka-dotted skirt how to find Dr. Echivari. The lady pointed up a steep hill and told Margarita to walk up it. And so she did, but instead of the dentist's office, she found *El lugar del olvido.* She saw driveways and fences hiding what might have been giant old houses; Margarita later told me she dreamed of living in one of these houses. (I didn't want to live in one of those houses at all—they reminded me of the cobwebby homes in scary movies like *The Amityville Horror.*) Instead of finding Dr. Echivari, Margarita found herself on top of a cliff, surrounded by Santa Monica Beach below. She noticed the swimmers, the runners, and the dog walkers. She couldn't stop staring. From then on, Margarita always went to the cliff top when she needed a happy, serene scene.

I wished she had told me what time she'd be back. I always worried, and Margarita knew this. I went inside and asked my parents what had happened, or at least their version of the story. And for the first time ever, when I really wanted them to say something, Mama and Papa remained silent. So I locked myself in my room and attempted to distract myself and finish my book.

It was nine at night when I finally turned the last page. I was eager to start a new book; I wasn't even thinking about Margarita. I went into the living room and there was still silence, that silence that I hated. That silence upset me as much as having a fish bone stuck in my throat. I turned on the TV to see if I could catch the second episode of *The Simpsons.*

When the clock turned ten, Papa finally spoke up and said, "*¿Adonde esta Margarita?*" He turned and gave me an accusing look as if he knew I was hiding something. "*¿Maria, tu sabes adonde esta tu hermana?*"

Though I knew exactly where she was and even directions for how to get there, I hesitated to answer. I had sworn to Margarita that I would never say anything about *El lugar del olvido.* I answered him: "No, Papa. She just left without saying a word." He knew I was lying, so I shamefully turned away. He gave me a familiar look, one that burned me from the inside out.

I suggested that my parents call Margarita's friends. Papa sighed and proceeded to call Margarita's boyfriend, her boyfriend's friends, and many others in and around our neighborhood. But no Margarita. The big hand of the old clock began moving faster. Hours passed like days, and at 2:30 AM, Papa and I grew weary. I tried desperately not to fall asleep, yet my body begged for a quick nap on the couch. What seemed like only a few minutes later, I opened my eyes and found myself in my bedroom. The alarm clock I got for Christmas blinked 3:45 AM I heard someone knocking at the door.

Who could be at the door before the rooster crowed *ca-cará-kiando*? I squeezed my pillow over my head. But wait, I said to myself: She's here! I got out of bed, still wearing the clothes from my birthday party, and ran toward the door. I found Papa in the hallway, and we both discovered Mama in the kitchen. Two police officers sat beside her with cups of coffee.

The officers stood up, and one of them said, "Good morning, Mr. Torres. Please sit down." I knew something bad had happened.

The taller of the officers was very thin, and his nametag read "Pedro Gonzales." With a deep voice, he said, "Your daughter has been in a car accident. She hit a pothole and lost control of her car. She then hit a tree."

"But when did this happen?" Mama asked with tears in her eyes.

A pit formed in my stomach. Margarita's accident was entirely my fault. I should have told Papa about *El lugar del olvido*. I cleared my throat, but before I was able to say anything, the other officer said, "Unfortunately, she passed away en route to the hospital."

We got into our blue Nissan and drove to East Los Angeles Hospital. When Papa turned on First Street to go down a hill, the car drove over a pothole, and he cursed. "Won't they ever fix these streets? A mouse has a better neighborhood!"

When we approached the hospital's driveway, Papa left the car in park with the engine still running. I got out of the car and ran through the big transparent doors, leaving my parents behind. I knew this hospital like the back of my hand—not only had I been born there, but my regular doctor, Dr. Waldman, who treated me for asthma, worked there too.

I found a nurse and asked her where my sister was. As she led me down an unfamiliar hallway, I thought to myself, I have never seen a dead person before.

We walked into a very big and very cold room. There were many gray shiny drawers—just like the ones I've seen on TV shows. They reminded me of how the Downtown skyscrapers looked, and I wondered if they were made of the same material. The doctor opened one of those big drawers and asked, "Is this your Margarita?" When I saw Margarita's pale face, which once had shown so much love for me, I couldn't help but run out of that freezer full of corpses.

I sat down in a chair, panting, with tears streaming down my cheeks and into my mouth; I could taste the saltiness of my tears. I noticed my parents, now with only one daughter left, filling out the necessary paperwork.

My parents and I piled back into the blue Nissan, and the engine roared over our silence. For the first time ever, I saw Papa cry. Like any typical macho man, he wasn't programmed to cry. We drove along Whittier Boulevard and took a left on First Street, when again, the car dipped into the same maddening pothole, but this time no one said anything. We reached home, obviously more empty without Margarita. I went into my room and cried myself to sleep.

Nearly a year after my sister's death, I still felt numb, and I dramatically thought of suicide. My life wasn't the same without Margarita—I wished so badly to be with her, unreasonably so. Mama worked two jobs so she was spending more time out of the house than in. Whenever I tried to talk to her, she would interrupt me and say it was time for her to go to work. Papa was a different story: he stopped going to work altogether. He did nothing but drink, sleep, and when he remembered, he would eat.

My birthday this year was very different. The day I turned fifteen, I went to the library on Cesar Chavez; I wished that I owned the entire place so I could take as many books home as I wanted. Later, as I approaching my front door, I remembered what it was like last year as I walked into the living room. No one shouted "Surprise!" this time.

Every day I did the same thing—wake up, go to school, come back home and feel sorry for myself. I no longer had friends; I felt isolated. I needed to talk to someone, but who would want to talk to me? I was unpopular, and my sister had died. With this thought and on this very sad birthday, I mourned the happy life I had once had.

I continued to nurture the same lonely despair. One day, I decided to stick around school after the bell rang. I walked around campus until I came upon an after-school club holding its meeting. I eavesdropped a little, and my interest was piqued. I walked in, and five students swiveled their heads to look at me. I went directly up to the teacher, used my most polite voice, and said, "Good afternoon, Mr. Rodriguez. I was wondering if I may join your club?" And he said, "Of course."

It was a creative writing club, and they met every Monday, Wednesday, and Friday from 3:15 to 4:30. There I learned that writing is not only a school chore, but it is also considered an art form. I didn't argue with this concept: Writing was exactly what I needed to express myself.

When I returned home that day, no one noticed that I was two hours late—Papa was drunk, and Mama was at work. I finished my homework, ate dinner, showered, and climbed into bed. The next day I followed the same routine, but somehow, now I felt a bit better.

My English teacher, Mrs. Dignam, gave this assignment to the class: Write about someone you admire. I considered Mama, how she probably suffered more than Papa and me. I barely considered Papa, because I had no spiritual connection with him. I decided to write about Margarita— about how much I missed her and how much I wished she were still here. I plotted this piece very carefully, writing every detail with such care. It felt like my sister was sitting right in front of me, giving me ideas. After I turned in the assignment, Mrs. Dignam gave me a curious look.

"Maria, can you please stay after class for a few minutes?" she said. The teacher dismissed everyone but me. What was this about, I wondered. It made me nervous to be singled out. I assumed that I had done something bad and that my punishment was going to be delivered. My palms were sweating, and I felt my face getting hotter.

To my surprise, Mrs. Dignam said with a smile, "Maria, what a great paper! There is so much promise in this. I hope you keep writing on your own."

When I heard this praise, I felt a huge weight lifted off my shoulders. I smiled and thanked her for her encouragement. As I walked home, feeling very proud of myself, I wondered how Margarita would have felt.

Before I went to sleep that night, I heard my parents fighting again; their argument followed the usual outline of topics they argued about, but this time it sounded a lot worse. Above all the screaming, I heard Mama yell, "Just hit me, why don't you?" Then I heard a bottle smash—into what, I don't know— and a loud silence followed. I tiptoed out of my room and saw Mama lying on the floor with a puddle of blood next to her head. She wasn't moving. When I saw Papa approaching me, I ran into my room and locked myself in.

Not knowing what to do, I started to cry uncontrollably. As I thought about how Mrs. Dignam had told me that I was actually good at something, I decided to write. I wrote a sentence expressing how I felt that very moment, and then I converted that into a poem. As the minutes passed, I challenged myself to write more and more, but instead of using the boring writing techniques I had used before, I wrote this poem a different way: I wrote it from the heart—my Spanish heart.

In the morning, I revisited the scene from the night before. I noticed

Papa sleeping on the sofa; Mama, inevitably, was at work. Before I left for school, I left my poem on the kitchen counter. I hoped that Mama would see it.

When I got home from school, Mama greeted me with tears in her eyes. She was always so sad, my Mama! Then I saw the poem in her hand. She threw her arms around me and whispered in my ear, "*Yo te prometo que desde este día en delante todo cambiara.*"

And I believed her.

WHEN HE PICKED ME UP
JESSICA JUAREZ

The bell just rang
    and the wind is blowing.

I play on the monkey bars
    and the blisters keep coming.

I turn around and what do I see—it's the truck that's supposed to
    pick me up.

I get in and the smell of Old Spice hits my nose
    I'm on cloud nine . . . or ten . . . or . . .

. . . all of a sudden the radio jolts me.

The sound of an old man's pain is going into
    my head and it's making me insane.

It's the guy that's on the radio—I remember the verse:
    "When you handed me those papers . . ."
        —the divorce, and all that pain.

Memories came back
I grew to understand the feeling he felt that his heart could not erase;
I started to feel his pain and all of a sudden it's not driving me insane.

I catch myself singing the song, too.

I catch myself wanting to hear the guy cry out more,
    and more,
        and more . . .

✳

As we arrive, the car shuts off
    and with it goes the man's pain.

I just look at this handicapped man in front of me
    and wonder: How can such a man be so strong?

Does his heart beat on?
    Or at least as well as mine?

I see him going up the stairs;
    I see him holding on as if he were holding on for dear life.

As I go in the house, he calls mama for a beer
    to drink away the guy's sorrow, as if it were his own.

As I watch in disappointment, he calls mama a second time
    and mama comes with another beer . . .
        and another . . .
            and another . . .

✳

As I was awakened from the old man's pain again
    I get up and as I walk out of my room.

I go downstairs for a sound has put me in
    a trance, it's the
Sound of an old man who had
    a heart broken
By hiding his pain by drinking.

Then his voice, "get me another"
    I see my mother
As I look in his
    eyes it's pain that catches my
Attention and the

trance begins; I don't stop staring.

For then I see his dreams for me
 clear as can be.

It's like a play or skit
 that is happening right in front of me.

There I am graduating from Roosevelt High and college.
 There I am graduating from UCLA, and I see my dream
 of becoming a lawyer.

All of a sudden I awake,
 and as I step outside I look from side to side
  and realize that what he asked is so hard
   and so high for a person living in such a place.

I go back inside and see the man swallow his pain
 as if every drink he drinks makes a memory go away.
  So as you can see, dreams as easy as these are
  hard for someone like me.

LONG WAY HOME
DAVID BLANCARTE

"It's the last stop kid"
those are the disgruntled words from the
voice of an angry bus driver trying to stay on schedule
"What . . . Oh"
I get off still a bit sleepy and confused
but I get off nonetheless
the sun is near setting and slowly sinking into
the horizon, but that's the only thing that's familiar
the streets have jumbled names and the people look
awfully hostile but I know what street I have to walk on
and walk I do, and pray I do
anything to better my chances of getting home
without any trouble, with my cell phone, CD player,
and urine still intact, still under my control
so I walk second-guessing every step
in fear of stepping on the wrong territory
but I walk;
the faster I walk, the sooner
I'll get to where I have to be without having to deal
with any of that "Where you from?" or "What you write"
from the local gangs

A ball bounces in front of me leaving me dumbstruck
I stall unaware of what I should do
since stopping the ball and picking it up could be
a matter of life and death depending on whose ball it is
since nowadays people get shot, stabbed, or killed for the
dumbest of reasons
all my thinking wastes enough time for the
half-flattened worn-out soccer ball to roll right past me
"Thanks a lot *******" are the words that

follow my slow reactions, from the mouth of
a seven-year-old brown kid as he runs into the middle of the
street to get his rolling sorry excuse of a ball
it struck me as rather funny just because he was little
and he was using words that he probably didn't even know the real
meaning behind
but . . .
sorta sad in the same way, since even though he may not know
the meaning behind it he still uses the word and those aren't
the kinds
of words I'd want to hear from the mouth of my future kids
or my little brother
a car on its way to pick up the driver's friends happened
to be speeding by, the boy never even looked
but luckily this time the driver did,
he swerved a bit and honked loudly but it was muffled
by the sound of his huge woofer bumping the latest reggaeton hit
the boy wasn't scared he just flipped off the driver
and the driver returned the gesture
and after I regained my composure I continued to
walk and the boy and his friends continued
to play, and the driver continued on his drive to
go pick up his friends, the whole ordeal was completely forgotten;
just like the rules that say you must look
both ways before you walk and that the speed limit
is 15 mph in residential areas

I walk on and the houses start to seem rather repetitive, all distinct
to an extent but used for the same reason
housing the same people, the same little brother
who will rat you out to your mom the moment
you step through the door, the same
unreasonable mother ready to shred your self-esteem
to pieces limb by limb, the same
defeated older sister who is always used as the
bad example and the epitome of what you're becoming according
to your mother, the same dad who only enters the house
to close his eyes in it, to be woken up to leave to work again the
next day, and most importantly

the cautious people who must lock themselves ·
in their houses, with bars on their windows, spikes on
their gates, and guns under their pillows
in order to feel safe, well at least to an extent . . .

The more I think about it the less foreign I feel
the more familiar the streets seem to be getting,
but is there a difference?
We're raised in the same place and raised in much the same way
and yet their presence makes me even fear
my own shadow on the dirty and cracked asphalt road in
fear that it might jack me
my feet are getting tired
and my shoulders droop as my heavy backpack
causes my body to sag in fatigue
but my goal is in reach, I can
almost taste the tender *carne asada* that
my mom has waiting for me at home

Turn the corner on my street after giving
a silent thanks to the cross on the empty
Baptist church with a huge For Sale sign on it,
my sore feet rejoice at the sight of my block
and my chest lets out a huge sigh of relief
I'm glad I'm back to the norm, back
to where I belong
the sun is setting over the
metro bridge and I begin to walk in the middle of the street
due to the large overflowing garbage bins that own the sidewalk
it sure feels great to be home
everyone knows me here, and I know where
it is safe to step, in case of emergency
home is close enough to protect me
under the Christmas angel ornament that hangs at the peak
of the roof of my South Central home
I see the familiar faces and they see me
but yet they don't acknowledge me, they don't ask
of my journey, they don't ask how my day was,
they just watch me pass by behind their spiked gates

and stare me down until I stare away
I open the black spiked gate on my house
I stare up at the angel ornament that's been there through
the seasons, I look at him expecting the warm feeling of home
but I don't receive it, because he's just an ornament
I open the door and turn the lights on
There's no *carne asada* waiting for me . . .

EXPLORING L.A.: IN AND OUT
FABIOLA AVILA

My L.A. has been a great part of my life. It is a place where my family loves to explore and try new things. When we are at home, the only things we ever talk about are school and work. When we're lucky enough to take a camping trip or go someplace new, we have more time to spend together and to learn new things about each other. We talk about everything.

One day we went in search of a waterfall. It was my mother's idea—a friend had told my mom about this beautiful place with a big waterfall that we should see. My parents and I were excited to see this place in the mountains near our home, so we drove forty-five minutes to a forest near Azuza. When we got to the main entrance to the park, the ranger gave us a map so that we wouldn't get lost.

We started our walk so happy and excited to see a new place that we had never known about before. I had never seen a big waterfall, and I expected to see one as tall as a building. My mom was happy to be getting exercise and having fun at the same time. I was grateful that my parents and I had the opportunity to share this experience and spend more time together.

While we were walking, we saw all kinds of birds, leaves, bugs, and other people around us. We talked about the various wild animals in nature and how different they were from the animals in the city. The birds in my neighborhood are only brown, but the ones that I saw in the forest were blue, green, red, yellow, and orange. My mother was terrified that we might see snakes, but luckily nothing that could hurt us crossed our path.

For an hour we went up hills, down hills, crossed little rivers, and then we arrived at the waterfall. To our surprise, it was not the beautiful waterfall that we had expected to see: it was a little pond with a miniature waterfall.

We sat there for a couple of minutes and admired this place that brought joy to us. Even though we did not think that it was all that wonderful, it was new to us; to me, the most important thing was spending time with the people that I love.

The waterfall reminded me about all the good times I've had in L.A. Even though I know that L.A. is not the best place to live because of the pollution and traffic, I grew up here and am glad that I could be a part of this wonderful place. In a perfect world, L.A. would be one happy place without gangs, where people wouldn't hate each other and kill people only because they are different looking. L.A. could be free of pollution, traffic, and people in their cars who yell at you to get out of their way.

Even though L.A. is not perfect, many people have a lot of things in common; strangers can get along and become friends even when they are from different cultures. I'm happy here because I have people who I know will always be there for me when I need them. My family is here, and I love them. I learn new things from them that I would never learn in other places. They are the people who have taught me to be the way I am today.

People sometimes take Los Angeles for granted and don't see all the wonderful places and things that the city has to offer a person like me. Going to the waterfall helped me to appreciate that L.A. has more things to see and do than you can imagine. Most people don't take the opportunity to take advantage of all of these things. You can't stay in L.A. forever; you have to go out and explore other places so you can learn to appreciate the different things that are out there. The people who take L.A. for granted are the ones who end up staying here; it's funny, because it's the same way with students who always say that they want to get out of L.A. and go far away, but somehow they always end up staying here. This might be because of their wrong choices or because they decide at the last minute that they don't want to leave.

I always hear people in L.A. say that the children are our future, and that's why they try to do everything for us so that we are able to succeed in life.

ACQUAINTANCE
EDGAR CONTRERAS

Tomorrow will be a wonderful day for Charlie the Bear. He is going to visit his cousin Earl, who happens to live in Los Angeles. Earl is a circus bear, and a very proud one, too. Charlie is starting his day by gathering some blackberries for his trip. Charlie lives high in the foothills, where there are many tall trees. There are people who live near the bottom of the mountain. Charlie wanders down sometimes to eat out of their trash cans.

"Hey Charlie! Looking good, man."

"Hey, what's up, Larry?" Larry is a raccoon who likes to think of himself as a very strong and brave bear. He is very nice and friendly, though. Larry asks Charlie, "So, what's your big brown fur doing up so early? Don't tell me that you are going to tell that rascal Eddie to stop stealing the fish that you leave in your den." Eddie is another bear who hunts regularly with Charlie.

"Larry, I know that it is not Eddie who is stealing my fish."

"Oh yeah? How do you know that, smart bear?"

"For starters, you are the only one who knows that I leave my fish hidden under a rock in my den."

"Whoa, whoa, whoa," exclaims Larry. "And how do you know that, *compadre*?"

"Well, Larry, you just told me that I leave my fish in my den. Plus your breath smells like salmon."

"Oh, I guess you caught me. You're not going to eat me, are you? You know I got a family."

"Well," says Charlie, "first of all, I don't eat my friends, and second of all, you don't have a family, you live with your girlfriend, who by the way would love to have a family with you if you weren't so stern."

"Charlie, believe me, a raccoon with six brothers and sisters knows about family life."

Charlie shifts his attention to the berries that he is picking.

Larry notices that Charlie is picking more berries than usual. "Hey Charlie, tell me, where are you going?"

"I'm going to visit my cousin Earl in the circus. I haven't seen him in years. He sent me a message via wing."

"Eagle or falcon?" asks Larry.

"Falcon, of course," Charlie replies.

"So what did he tell you?"

"That he wanted me to see the big city. I leave tomorrow morning. I will follow the path of that big road, the freeway"—Larry looks where Charlie is pointing—"and go towards those big buildings there."

Larry sees the city, and it looks so beautiful. It seems like an island that is just floating. Charlie is also looking at the buildings. He is picturing himself walking down the streets of Los Angeles. He likes the idea of going to a new place, and as he pictures himself in the city, his eyes glow with excitement and anticipation.

The Journey

The next morning, Charlie wakes up early. He gathers the collected berries and puts them in a leaf, then he folds the leaf and ties it to his neck with a piece of vine. Charlie makes his steady way down the mountain. He is now close to a neighborhood; he reaches the first houses in twenty minutes. "It must be a Saturday," thinks Charlie, "because there seems to be no one in the houses." He looks around and sees the clean streets with perfect short green grass, and different stores with nice cars parked nearby. It takes him about forty-five minutes to reach the bottom of the mountain and get on the main road. Finally, Charlie sees some people walking by. It is a family of four; they are going to a restaurant, and they look very happy.

Charlie turns to the path ahead. He is walking beside the freeway where there are lots of trees. Once a bear gets started on a journey, he never looks back. It is a bear's belief that if you look back to the place you are leaving, you will never be able to return. To look back would bring man's curse: the wilderness will be destroyed by businessmen who want to build a McDonald's or a Burger King in the homes of animals.

As Charlie walks, he begins to notice some peculiar things. First, he notices that the road is full of trash. "Wow, I guess one of those big dump trucks must have had a hole in it and the trash flew out," he thinks. Then Charlie feels his eyes stinging. He senses a disturbance in the air. "Something is not right here," he tells himself, but he keeps on moving. Charlie is only a few miles away from downtown Los Angeles. "Ah, what is that smell? It is horrible." What he smells is

Illustration by Evelyn Flores

similar to the smell of the bad trash he does not eat when he is down near the houses back in the foothills. Up close, Los Angeles no longer looks like a floating island.

Two Worlds, One Planet

Charlie hits the center of Los Angeles. He is in the middle of those tall buildings and is overwhelmed with wonder. He sees people walking by, and they look just like the people back in the foothills. The people are well dressed, but he sees stress in their faces. He also notices that people move much faster than his friends back home—they walk as if something is chasing them. Earl has already sent Charlie directions: he is supposed to follow the strongest smell. At first Charlie does not understand what Earl is talking about, but then he gets it. The strongest smell comes from the east. It is the smell of unwanted trash again.

Tragedy Averted

Charlie is distracted by the buildings and the people, so he does not see what is ahead of him. Suddenly, a loud noise makes him turn around. The sound of screeching tires is unfamiliar—he does not know that a car is heading straight towards him.

"Hey, you crazy bear. What the hell do you think you are doing? I almost turned you into roadkill! I have enough tickets for turning pigeons into windshield soup! You hear me, you furball?"

"Oh man," says Charlie, "I've got to be more careful." As he gathers himself, he realizes that he is in a different world. Charlie is no longer standing in front of nice-looking buildings, full of nicely dressed business-men. He is now in what appears to be a wasteland where unwanted things are taken. Charlie is on what most of us know as *los callejones*, a place where people go to buy clothes, toys, and all kinds of things that give meaning to the phrase "You get what you pay for." In most cases, you don't pay much.

"What kind of place have I stepped into now?" Charlie sees many things that do not make sense to him. He cannot understand why there is such a difference between this street and the one behind him. The streets are black here, not gray as they are behind him. The people are not walking around in business suits. Instead, they are all sleeping on the ground, just as Charlie would in a cave.

"But these are people," Charlie says to himself, "not bears!" Charlie has never seen a human sleep on the floor—he did not even know that humans *could* sleep on the floor. All these people have a very strong smell, too.

It is early in the morning and some of them are beginning to awaken. Charlie notices their expressions. He sees sorrow and suffering. Charlie is no city bear, but he knows that these people are outcasts from human society. Charlie is very smart. Even though most of his friends disagree with him, he believes that humans have a society where there are leaders, followers, and outcasts just like in a wolf family. Charlie knows about outcasts because he has talked to many old bears who have been defeated by younger bears and chased out of their own territories. Charlie understands the cruelty that can befall any animal as he ages. "But," he thinks, "these people don't look old." As a matter of fact, many of them look young. Charlie feels something deep in his soul, a feeling new to him. He does not know if it is sorrow or anger, or maybe a mix of the two. One of the people speaks to Charlie. This man's name is Johnson, and he knows a lot about his surroundings. "Hey man," Johnson says, "you escape from some kind of zoo? Ya not gonna eat me, are ya?"

Charlie laughs to himself. Larry has said the same thing to him, so this remark makes Charlie lower his guard. Charlie tells Johnson all about his trip.

"Just call me John," the man says. "Everyone who is my friend here calls me that, and if you not my enemy, then you my friend."

Talking to a complete stranger is something new for Charlie, but with John he feels safe.

"So you saying you come down here all the way from the foothills?" John asks. "Wow—you know the foothills is very different from where you is right now?"

Charlie thinks to himself, "You're right." Charlie also knows that he has to keep moving, and even though Charlie trusts John, he does not want to stay in this particular place when night comes.

The Bridge

Charlie crosses a bridge where a river drifts underneath. At first glance the river looks clean, but when Charlie stops and sniffs the air, he knows differently. He just smelled the L.A. River, and when Charlie smells the dead river he does not want to think of it or smell it any longer, because it scares him to know that humans can pollute such a beautiful thing as a river. It is dark, and Charlie has no idea where he is.

Charlie wakes up very hungry; his stomach is making noises. He has run out of berries and needs to find food. Charlie is in a residential neighborhood, so he looks for food in trash containers. "Man," he says to himself, "there is so much trash here but nothing that I can eat."

Charlie accidentally drops a trash can. Big mistake, because a second later, out comes a screaming woman with a broomstick. Charlie hears words coming out of the woman's mouth, but they do not make sense: Charlie thinks she is crazy. The woman is not crazy, she is just speaking Spanish. Charlie thinks that the woman is going to clean the street, which is very dirty, but the woman gives him such a hard blow to the head with the broom that as he runs, his paws keep crossing each other. Charlie thinks, "Oh man, these people have more trash in the street than they do in their trash cans, and one reason is because they use their brooms to hit innocent hungry bears instead of cleaning the street."

Eventually Charlie stops in front of another bridge. He sees bushes on the other side, and he recognizes the leaves. He says to himself, "Berries grow on those bushes." He decides to go over and try his luck, but as soon as he starts walking, he smells something horrible. Charlie smells death. He reluctantly looks in the direction of the smell, and what he sees scares the fur off him: lying in plain sight is a black shape full of flies and maggots. The smell is unbearable; Charlie can't even move. He does not understand why this dead animal has been abandoned. Charlie cannot bear it, so he moves on.

Charlie gathers his courage and decides to head for the bushes. He is happy with what he finds. After he eats he feels better, although he now realizes that he is lost. He looks back at the bridge and decides to stay here for a couple of days, even though he won't get to visit his cousin Earl. Charlie thinks to himself, "I am lost and tired, and I am going to find a place to rest here." He makes a den in a park close to the bridge. The park is very big, and Charlie makes a den in a part where people never go. Charlie is now a little terrified of humans.

For about a week Charlie hangs around the bridge and its disgusting trash. One day, as Charlie is crossing the bridge, he steps on an empty potato chip bag. "Hmm," he thinks, "I wonder why people can't wait until they get home to throw trash like this away." Then Charlie gets an idea: "I can clean this place up; I have nothing else to do."

The next day Charlie wakes up early and heads to the bridge. He begins by picking up the small things first, things like potato chip bags. Then he moves up to the bigger, heavier items like tires and pieces of wood. He also finds a couch that was apparently thrown out the night before. As Charlie moves the couch, he tells himself, "It's a good thing that bears are strong or else I don't know what I would do." The sun is right over his head. He decides to take a little break and goes to collect some berries. Then, as he heads back to the bridge, he is astonished to see how different it looks. "Wow," Charlie exclaims. "This place actually looks like a bridge."

Charlie feels tired and for a moment thinks of heading home. Then he tells himself, "If I start something, I have to end it; it's a bear's way." So he continues his work all through the night. He not only has to remove the trash from the bridge but also take it uphill to a trash container. He thinks how ironic it is that the trash is always being dumped on the bridge when there is a big blue container here, just a couple of blocks away.

Finally, Charlie is finished. He takes one more good look at the bridge right before he heads to his den in the park, and as he sees what he has accomplished, he can't help but smile.

The Next Day

The next day Charlie wakes up late. He is still a little tired from the hard work of the night before, and his muscles ache. He decides to go back downtown to talk to John.

Charlie arrives at about noon. He finds John looking through trash cans, fishing for plastic bottles to trade for money. Charlie quickly remembers the day that he was hit in the head with the broom; he is a little concerned that John will be hit with a broom as well.

As soon as John spots Charlie, his face loses the dark, stern look of a tired man and breaks into a smile. Charlie tells John what happened after his departure. He mentions how he got lost and decided that it would be impossible to find his cousin Earl. Charlie also mentions the broom and then the most important thing of all, which is why he has come here: he tells John all about the bridge and how he cleaned it. He finishes his story, and John asks, "So ya want me to clean this big city? Is that what ya tryin' to say?" Charlie tells John that things look much better when they are clean and that he should think about it. Charlie also mentions that dangerous bacteria thrive in trash cans.

Charlie heads back to the bridge and sees lots of children walking across it, and he is astonished. He cannot imagine that kids routinely walked over a bridge that was as filthy as this one had been just the day before. Charlie watches as they walk, and then he sees something familiar in the hands of some of the children: potato chip bags like the one he cleaned up the night before. "Now I know where all those bags come from, but why don't these kids just wait until they get home and then throw away their trash properly?" Charlie ponders this for a moment. He decides to wait and see just who throws the first piece of trash.

Eventually, he sees it. It is a kid laughing with his friends. He drops an empty bag of chips to the ground. To Charlie, it looks as if the bag has simply fallen by mistake. As fewer and fewer kids cross the bridge, Charlie feels relieved, because there is only one piece of trash on the ground.

Then Charlie sees a couple of kids coming from the other side of the bridge, one big kid and one younger one. "They are the last ones," he thinks. The kids are carrying bags of chips and cans of soda and other items that could potentially end up on the bridge as trash. As he watches, the bigger kid throws his can of soda and bag of chips into the street, which seems awfully intentional to Charlie. The smaller kid tells the bigger one not to do that, which catches Charlie off guard. "Hey, man," the kid says, "why do you throw your garbage here? You know you're making this place seem more like a dump. We already live in a messed-up city, and you're making it look trashy and nasty."

The bigger kid responds, "Hey, dude, why you tripping? It's just a little bit of trash. It's not like I'm throwing furniture like most people do, and besides, look over there." The boy points at the bag of chips that was dropped earlier. "You see," he says, "somebody already threw something here before I did."

The next day Charlie wakes up with an idea: he is going to put a theory of his to the test. He waits until noon when all the kids pass over the bridge. He watches carefully and expectantly as the kids get closer to where he is hiding. Nothing happens; twenty minutes pass by, and still nothing. Then Charlie spots a bunch of boys walking with soda cans and potato chip bags in their hands. He watches again very carefully. One of the kids drops a can of soda, but he seems unaware of it. Just like the first time, this kid did not throw the soda can intentionally; it just fell from his hand and he did not notice.

Charlie waits for this first group of kids to pass before he goes to work. He picks up the can of soda and quickly goes back to his place behind a tree. Charlie watches as the rest of the kids walk over the bridge, and just as he had expected, no trash is thrown. His theory is that if there is no trash for the kids to see on the bridge, no one will throw trash. People respond to what they see, so if a person sees a trash-filled street or bridge, they will most likely throw their own garbage there as well. When the kids passing over the bridge today saw a clean bridge, they did not throw trash because they didn't want to be guilty of making the place dirty. One person's actions can, and in many cases do, influence other people. Charlie goes to sleep that night with a big smile on his face.

The next day Charlie wakes up to hear loud noises coming from the bridge. "It sounds like a swarm of bees," he thinks, but it is not a swarm of bees, but rather a swarm of people. People have noticed that the bridge is clean and have decided to investigate. Charlie emerges from his hideout and goes toward the crowd, but as soon as he reaches them he wishes he hadn't come. A woman begins to scream in a language that is indecipherable but very familiar to Charlie all the same: it is the same woman who hit him in the head the day he was looking for food in the trash container. As soon as Charlie recognizes the woman, his head begins to ache. He stops dead in his tracks and does not dare to take another step forward. Then a man yells to the frantic woman, "*Hey, que traes vieja loca?*"

The woman shows the man one of her fingers. Charlie does not know what this means, but he guesses that it must be something bad, because then the man puts his right hand up and folds his fingers down, sort of like making a fist but going only halfway. Another man asks Charlie if he knows who cleaned the bridge.

"I cleaned it," answers Charlie, expecting recognition.

"Oh yeah, and who the hell told you to do it?" screams out the man.

"Nobody told me to do it. I just did it because this place looked like a dump and I thought it would look better if I cleaned it up."

"What are you saying, you dumb bear? That we can't clean up our own bridges?"

"Well, can you?" Charlie asks. This infuriates the man. He looks hard at Charlie.

"Why don't you go back to your own place, bear; you don't belong here."

"Yeah," says the crowd in unison.

Charlie's response: "I will be leaving soon."

"No," says the man, "you will be leaving now."

Charlie looks into the eyes of the man and he sees fear there. He turns around and begins his journey back to the forest. Then he hears a tiny voice. "Hey, the bear is right, the bridge does look much better." It is the small boy who was trying to stop his friend from littering. "I think the bear is right," says another man. "We should not allow our streets and bridges to be so dirty. I mean, I don't tolerate a dirty house, so why should I tolerate a dirty bridge where my son walks five days a week?"

"Yeah," the people call out.

"From now on," the man yells, "we will have a clean bridge and a clean neighborhood."

Charlie decides that it is time to leave Los Angeles, but before he can go home, he wants to say good bye to John, the only friend he has made on his journey. As Charlie leaves, he hopes the people have learned a lesson. You should not throw trash simply because you see other people do it. If you pick something up instead of throwing something to the ground, you should give yourself a pat on the back, because you have just done a good thing. Charlie picked up a piece of trash thrown accidentally by a child, and because of his actions the rest of the kids refrained from throwing things on the bridge. They saw a clean bridge and so they kept it a clean bridge.

Illustration by Evelyn Flores

The End of Things

Charlie walks downtown, where he looks for John. He says to himself, "He should be around here." By this time he should be out collecting cans." Charlie goes to where John sleeps, but the corner looks different. A man approaches Charlie from behind. "I've seen you here before," he tells him, "talking to John." As the man says this, a shadow comes over his face.

"Can you tell me where he is? I need to say good-bye to him."

"I'm afraid John isn't with us any longer."

"What do you mean?"

"I mean he is in a better world, a place where he will be treated as a human being."

"What? How did this happen? I just talked to him a few days ago."

"Well, it seems that he got a bacterial disease—it happens a lot around here from eating food that has gone bad. You, a bear, can eat anything, but not us. We weren't meant to eat garbage or rotten meat, no sir." The man stops talking, lost deep in thought.

Charlie turns around before the tears reach his cheeks. There is nothing more to do but head home.

Back to the Beginning

Charlie is sad because of John's death, but he is also happy that he made a difference for the people who use the bridge. Having a clean street is like a window to who you are.

It takes Charlie about two days to get from Los Angeles to the foothills, in part because he is extremely tired. Charlie came to Los Angeles to see the wonders of the city but found the complete opposite. He saw that there are different kinds of people, as different as all the kinds of animals in the foothills, and he learned that not all people have beds to sleep in.

Charlie is about a quarter of a mile from the foothills, but then he stops dead in his tracks. He smells something familiar that should not be here, not here in the foothills. He smells trash, just like in Los Angeles, the same trashy, nasty smell.

"No!" Charlie roars, and then he hears machinery. He looks towards the mountain where his den is hidden in the trees, but he can't even see it because a gray cloud has consumed the whole mountaintop. But it's not a cloud; clouds aren't so black. It's smoke. Yes, smoke is rising from the mountain. It is not a fire, however—Charlie knows this right away. He says to himself, "If it's a fire, then all the animals would be running down the mountain. I don't see a single creature, not even birds hovering above." Charlie is very worried and decides to investigate. He walks up the mountain and notices that a line of trees has been cut, as if to make a path for something. Something big. Something bigger than twenty bears.

When Charlie gets to the top of the mountain, he sees what has happened. The mountaintop has been turned into a dump site. Not a single tree is standing. Gigantic tractors work, digging up dirt to bury the nasty, smelly trash. Charlie worries about his friends. "Larry, Eddie, where have you gone to?" Charlie does not know what to do. He no longer has a home or any friends. That night he goes to sleep right beside the freeway in a patch of trees.

To Sleep You Go

Charlie wakes up the next morning to a noisy world. It sounds like people, yes, people talking really loud.

Charlie feels very tired and does not know what to do or where to go. He is very sad because he does not know what happened to his friends when the mountain was invaded. He wonders: Are they still alive? Did they get out of the way in time? What will I do now?

Charlie walks along the patch of trees. He sees a multitude of people just a few hundred feet from him. They are the residents of the foothills. The people are holding objects in the air. They are talking all at the same time, saying the same thing in unison. Charlie moves closer because he wants to know what the commotion is about. When he gets close enough to comprehend what the people are saying, he is shocked to his paws.

They are chanting, "Stop cutting down the trees."

Meanwhile, another group of people yells, "Our home is not a dump; take this trash out of our homes." A lot of people have gathered to protest and demand that the tractors go away and that their homes be left alone. Then Charlie sees some familiar faces: many of the people who are protesting to protect the forest are the people from the bridge in Los Angeles. They're here defending his home from becoming a big trash container.

"Hey, look, it's the bear. He made it," screams a man. "Hey bear, you OK?"

Charlie walks up to the crowd once he hears the man.

"What are you all doing here?" asks Charlie.

"We're here to help you out. We heard on the news that the foothills were going to be turned into a dump. At first we didn't pay any attention, but somebody informed us that you had come from the foothills, so we decided to lend a hand."

It was John's friend who told people that Charlie had come from the foothills; apparently John told his friend where Charlie came from before he died. Charlie says, "That John."

Charlie's home is spared—the mayor cannot stand the pressure from all the protesters. The foothills will stay nice and clean, thanks to the people from Los Angeles. And oh yes, Larry, Eddie, and all of Charlie's

friends are still alive and well. They got out of the hills just in time and
hid in an abandoned house nearby. Long ago, the house belonged to
Joseph and Margaret Willard, the parents of a man named Johnson
Willard: John.

LUZ ELENA, THE GHOST STORY TELLER
GABRIELA BAUTISTA

The story that I am about to tell is not an ordinary ghost story like the ones you might read in books or hear from friends. This story is about real spirits in real life. These things happened to my grandmother, they are stories about the supernatural, and it's up to you to decide whether or not to believe them.

My grandmother, Luz Elena Salazar, grew up in La Piedad de Cabadas in Mexico. During the early 1900s, like my grandmother's family, much of Mexico's population was living in poverty. My grandmother's father, Pablo Salazar, was a very poor man who worked in the fields to support his huge family. There were times when he couldn't afford anything to eat. What he and his family didn't know was that they were about to become the richest people in their village.

One day Pablo found a pot of gold inside an abandoned *hacienda*. It was said that it could have belonged to the *hacendados*[1] from the time of the Mexican Revolution; many *hacendados* had so much money that, instead of depositing it in banks, they preferred to dig a hole and bury it for better protection. After Pablo discovered the pot of gold, however, problems began to occur.

Pablo was elected president of his village and bought many acres of land, but something strange and evil arose from that land. Deaths, problems, and unexplained things began happening: the pot of gold was cursed. From that time on Luz Elena began to see spirits. She had a sixth sense.

Whenever I visited my grandmother, my siblings, cousins, and I would beg her to tell us her stories. Excitedly, we would ask her, *"Abuelita, diganos sus historias de cuando estaba en México de las cosas espantosas que le sucedían."*[2] It was usually at night when everyone would gather closely around, listening intently to her chilling words. My grandmother would be lying down on the bed or sometimes sitting on the couch. I would focus directly on her hand gestures as she described how the ghost or monster looked; her mouth moved up and down as she whispered the stories. She was so descriptive that I could picture the creature and actually smell the scenery.

My grandmother would start off in a low, mysterious voice, "The day I saw La Llorona[3] I was pregnant with Gloria, my second child. My family and I were staying in La Granja Aurora or La Casa Grande. It was approximately 12 AM and everyone was asleep, but I woke up to a weird noise outside. The noise became louder and louder until it was unbearable; it sounded like two cats fighting. It was so frightening. I got up as quickly as I could from the squeaky bed—you see, I was willing to investigate, so I crept close to the window. And you know what I found?"

We all leaned forward, waiting to hear the answer.

"Absolutely nothing, so I got really nervous. Then an even louder noise came from outside. A woman was shouting her lungs out: "*Ay, mis hijos.*" I panicked! About five minutes passed, and the noise grew louder and louder. It got so close that I even felt the woman's breath on the back of my neck. I went and stood next to the window, and suddenly a woman appeared, staring right at me through the window, screaming, "*Ay, mis hijos.*" I froze: it was La Llorona in the flesh. She was very tall, wore a white gown, and was floating in the air. She had beautiful long black hair, but I was not able to see her face. After a blink she was gone, leaving no trace of herself."

Ever since my grandmother was a child, spirits followed her. It didn't matter if she was in La Piedad or Los Angeles; she would always attract the supernatural. When she was living in La Piedad, her father bought a house that was haunted by *duendes*,[4] which they did not know when they purchased it. My grandma told me about them.

"They were such troublemakers: every night they would come out while we were asleep and take away our blankets and throw them out the window, pull our hair and bother us all night. The *duendes* were tiny little things, real ugly and fast, but most of all, really scary. My family was tired of those trolls. We all hated them.

"One day we decided to move out; my father bought another house, and we were glad to be leaving. When we were packing the last of our belongings, my mother Angelina asked me, 'Luz, go get the broom from inside the house.' Before I had time to answer, someone else responded: '*Yo aca la llevo.*'[5] It was a *duende*! After all that, the *duendes* ended up moving to the new house with us!"

In 1989 my grandmother moved to Los Angeles, but she never kept the same home for long. In every house spirits would try to communicate with her. The spirits bothered her most when she was alone.

At thirty-three, my grandmother was diagnosed with diabetes. The disease took its toll, causing her to lose her eyesight. Even though her sight was gone, her ears were more sensitive than ever, and she was able to capture the smallest sounds. When I would visit my grandmother, I'd ask her, "Who scared you today?" She would respond with a frightened expression: "Oh, this person did, so and so . . ." In all her different homes, her room was always the coldest in the house. When she was alone in the house, spirits would whisper in her ear and blow on her face to get her attention; she would get really scared and tell them to leave her alone. Other times, as she tried to sleep, she could feel someone sitting next to her bed. The spirits would try to take advantage of her because of her blindness.

When my grandmother was hospitalized due to a wound on her leg, the diabetes complicated her recovery, and her leg was amputated. During her recovery I visited her in the hospital, and she would retell her stories. She would also give me home remedies to cure my animals, like washing them with special soaps to cure their skin illnesses.[6] Her love of animals inspired me to want to become a veterinarian.

While she was in the hospital, my grandmother saw her mother-in-law who had passed away the year before. My grandmother didn't really explain why her mother-in-law was there, but maybe it was a sign of her own destiny. She was sent home from the hospital and given only a small chance of survival. During her final days, she would call out the names of relatives who had passed away.

After my grandmother's death, some of her loved ones told stories about seeing her both in their dreams and while they were awake. One day her son Manuel saw her standing next to him, holding a Bible, with both of her legs healthy and whole again. Others saw her, too: now she'd become a spirit.

My cousin Daniela, who lives in Mexico, said that she saw Grandmother, whole again and smiling, repeating "Daniela, Daniela." Many other family members say that she visits them in their dreams, saying, "*nomas me dejaron salir un ratito.*"[7] These experiences were much less scary than what my grandmother had once said she'd do to me. She told me that after her time came, she would return and pull my legs while I was sleeping. I'd plead with her, scared: "*Abuelita, no me vaya a asustar, por favor.*"[8] She would just laugh while I shivered in horror.

After my grandmother's death, my family and I would gather in her house and share these stories. I remember hating to stay alone in her bedroom, the last place my grandmother took a breath, because I felt she was watching my every step. My cousin Alma said that near the anniversary of my grandmother's death, she felt her presence in that same room, felt the coldness, the vibration, and heard her complaining loudly of pain, over and over again in the night.

I am proud to say that I am the first one in my family who has written down my grandmother's stories. Now these stories are not just part of Mexico—they're part of Los Angeles as well, and will be retold. My grandmother, Luz Elena, after telling so many ghost stories herself, has now become a story to tell.

One day not long ago, about 3 AM, my sister Fabiola and I were deeply asleep when a vibration woke me. I heard loud footsteps dragging across the room. I felt a strong energy coming towards me and the presence of someone looking down at me. I got goose bumps from the tip of my toes to the top of my head as the energy passed through me, but when I opened my eyes, there was absolutely nothing in the room.

Something inside me told me that it could have been my grandmother coming to visit from beyond. A week later, my sister shocked me by telling me about her experience of that same night. It wasn't like her typical experience with the supernatural; no one sat on her bed or whispered in her ear. This time it was stronger than ever before: she had also felt someone looking at her and heard footsteps. Now I knew it wasn't just my imagination playing games with me—both of us couldn't have been dreaming.

I guess we will never know what it was, but I know one thing for sure: three days after this incident, I swear I heard a whispering that sounded just like my grandmother's voice directly in my ear. Maybe one day, if our paths cross, I will tell you what she said.

NOTES

1. Landlords.

2. "Grandma, can you tell us your scary stories from when you lived in Mexico?"

3. As legend has it, La Llorona drowned her children and herself in Rio Lerma and haunts all those who live near the river. My grandmother's ranch, La Granja Aurora, was on Rio Lerma's banks.

4. Hobgoblins.

5. "I already got it."

6. The weirdest thing happened the same day that my grandmother passed away: My two dachshunds, my sister's poodle, and my aunt's parakeet died within hours of her, with the same symptoms (vomiting blood) and just as painfully. My grandmother didn't want to die, and the pets seemed to fight their sudden deaths with similar fear and passion.

7. "They just let me out for a little while."

8. "Grandma, please don't scare me."

QUIETLY WISHING
ESPERANZA MENDEZ

My father grew up in a really poor village in a rocky and mountainous area of Mexico where the houses were made out of mud. It was a scary place because dangerous animals roamed at night. For these reasons, my father decided to immigrate to the United States; he really wanted a better place to live and a better job to support his family. His brother had gone before him, so my father decided to give it try. A year later he succeeded in entering the U.S., and he then came back. Without much time to waste, he decided to take us with him, but he realized that this time it wouldn't be as easy as it had been for him alone.

My parents had three children: my sister Patricia, my brother, and me. I was four years old, Patricia was six, and Armando was one. There were big risks in coming to the U.S.; if we walked, we would probably get lost. And babies have lots of needs: you have to feed them, change them, and put them to sleep. Instead of the whole family traveling together, my parents decided it would be less difficult and safer to take just my brother initially.

The three of them left our small town, which doesn't even appear on a map, then from there went to Tijuana—once you reach Tijuana you really have to make up your mind about what you're about to do. There, people just come out of nowhere and ask if you're going to the U.S. Some people are not honest; they are really persuasive and try to trick you by saying they will take you across the border, but that is not always true. Sometimes they'll start to take people across, but then they turn their backs and just leave them there, lost in the mountains or desert, after they've taken their money and all their valuables. It's like you're selling your life.

Luckily, my parents didn't have to go through that. They had a friend who knew people who were dedicated to helping people cross the border. This person has to bring many people across, and he has the responsibility to deliver all those lives safely.

I was scared, even though I didn't know what was going on. At four years old, you just want to be attached to your parents, to be safe and receive their love, but one day I woke up and my parents were gone. I tried to find some explanation, but there were too many questions and no answers. I had to stay behind with my grandmother and my sister. My grandmother was the only mother I had. I lived an ordinary life.

Six years went by. One day I came home from school and was told that I had to go a faraway place—my sister and I were going to Los Angeles to be with our parents. I asked myself: Why? What did I do? So many questions popped into my head out of nowhere, and I felt too many feelings that can't be described. Just hearing those words—"Los Angeles"— made me excited at first. At the same time I was scared. I had heard that L.A. was nothing like Mexico. The reason I was so excited was because I was going to see my parents for the first time since they had left us behind. I had no idea what my mom and dad would be like, because seeing a person in a picture is not the same as seeing them in real life. But then on second thought, I was thinking so many bad things about my parents; I used to ask myself why they had decided to leave us behind. For me, going to L.A. was like coming back to life in another place.

I remember back when I was nine or ten years old, I would hear stories about L.A., so many different people saying so many different things I didn't know what to believe. They described good things about L.A., things that would make you want to go there right away, as if it were no more difficult than going to your next-door neighbor's house.

I didn't want to come to the U.S. at first, because I knew my life was going to change completely. But even if I didn't want to come here I had to: my grandmother was suffering from a heart condition, and so I had to join my parents. It had been decided—the next day my sister and I were to begin our journey northward. I also heard many things could happen during the crossing, but ultimately you either die, or you make it safely.

It was exciting at first to be riding on a bus to a faraway place, seeing different landscapes on the way. However, leaving my grandmother behind felt like leaving a piece of me. It made me want to go back and get what I lost. It was very painful, because I knew that it was going to be a long time before I saw my grandma again, if ever, and this thought made me feel terrible and want to cry. But I had to go on—I wanted to be strong and to show others that I was doing something great. I put the painful thoughts behind me and decided that coming to the U.S. would be fun. I imagined all the people I was going to see on the way there, all the different places I'd never been and would discover for the first time.

I thought that boarding a plane would be the best part of all. I had never seen a plane so close up, only in pictures, and the thought of actually going inside one and sitting there for hours—God, I felt so excited. Sometimes I thought I was dreaming; having two feelings at once, excitement and fear, is a very crazy experience. I just wanted to feel good, so I kept thinking good things about coming here and meeting new people and learning a different language. And there was so much I did not know: Where would I live? What would it look like? And school: I thought about school. Would it be the same as my old school? I had no idea at all. The only thing I could do was wait, keep thinking about new things, and go along with whatever happened.

But then I realized I never really wanted to come to Los Angeles in the first place. I wanted to turn back and run like I had never run before. On the way here I was trying to memorize the route so I could find my way back, because I really wanted to return to my grandmother. I was afraid to meet my parents and nervous about talking to them in person for the first time in all these years.

When I finally saw them, everything was different. I asked myself, "Are they my parents?" They looked so different from what I had thought and what I had seen in photographs; this surprised me, because obviously people's appearances change, but somehow I expected them to look just like the pictures I had of them. At first I didn't know if they were my parents, but talking to them just felt right.

We started talking about many things. How was our family still in Mexico? How were we feeling? What had happened the last few days? How was the journey? And from that conversation, I knew for sure that they were my parents. Although everything fit just right, I didn't feel comfortable or trusting yet. I thought to myself that luckily I was here safe and that nothing bad had happened on my way to Los Angeles, and, well, I was just going to adjust to being here, little by little.

It was nighttime when we got to our house and I was really tired—all I wanted was to sleep and wake up and find that this was all a dream. I wanted to wake up the next day to find I was back in Mexico, living with my grandmother like before. I closed my eyes and I went to sleep without thinking about anything else.

I clearly remember that when I woke up, I realized that everything I remembered from the day before was reality, not a dream. The first thing I did was to look around at every corner and every wall in the room. There was a picture of smiling kids, and right away I knew that one of them was my brother Armando, who had come to L.A. with my parents. The other two faces were my little brother and my sister, who were born here in the U.S. I knew that I was going to meet a lot of people that day, which I did: aunts and uncles, cousins, and neighbors. It was strange to meet all those new people, but there was nothing I could do—this experience wasn't a dream, no matter how much I wanted it to be.

After we were introduced to so many people that day, my parents took my sister and me shopping. I thought it was cool that I was going out to experience the real Los Angeles, to finally see it for myself with my own eyes. But even so, I didn't really want to go—I just wanted to stay where I was, wishing to go back to Mexico. Looking at my sister Patricia, I saw that she seemed happy. I didn't know how she felt on the inside, but just looking at her motivated me to give this a chance, to look forward and to think that all this could be a big adventure, this exploration of a new world.

My first impression of L.A. was that it was a very busy city; everyone seemed to be in a hurry. And it was really noisy. Everybody just seemed to be minding their own business. There were different people from many races, which I had never seen before. Many cars were going many different ways, just as the people were doing.

Somehow, I didn't think I liked L.A. Maybe it was the way the city looked. It was very different from where I had lived in Mexico. In Mexico, everyone knows their neighbors, who they are and where they are. Here in L.A., people seemed afraid to talk to each other, or maybe they just didn't care; they just looked concerned with their own doings.

From that moment on, I wanted to go back to Mexico. I thought about the things that I would have been doing if I were back home. And I also asked myself, What would my grandma be doing right now? Where would she be? Does she miss us? How would she feel about this place? I was so worried about her; I didn't want her to be alone. I just wanted to go back!

I felt like crying. I knew that I was not going back to Mexico and that I was going to stay here for some time. All I wanted was to go back to Mexico, but crying wasn't going to get me there. So I swallowed my tears and thought about what would happen next. I wait, still wishing all the time to go back.

THE OTHER PIECE OF MY LIFE
PATRICIA MENDEZ

Waiting in a place I had never been, waiting for people I hadn't seen for seven years, made me feel something I hadn't felt in years, something I couldn't describe. I didn't know if I was nervous, happy, or both.

My sister Esperanza and I had traveled from Tijuana to Los Angeles to be reunited with our parents after many years. At first I was scared, for a lot of reasons big and small: I thought, why am I here with strange people? What if they go to the wrong house? What if we get lost and I don't find my parents? What if I don't get any of the new opportunities they say I will have in Los Angeles? Plus, I didn't know what I was going to say or do when my parents arrived.

Knowing they are finally going to be with me again makes me happy, and nervous too. I can't help but wonder if they are excited about our being together again. Or maybe they are mad? I am happy that they are finally going to be with us again. Why am I so worried? Will they remember me? Will they still love me after seven years, seven years without my being able to help them as most mothers do? Are they happy to meet their parents, who they don't know anymore? Are they going to cry? Will I cry too? The first moment will tell me everything. The only thing I know is that my dream has come true: we are going to be together again and be as happy as any family can be. I know I have to tell them my reasons for leaving them. So many people told me that we would find new opportunities and a better life in L.A. I wanted us to all come together, but we didn't have enough money; because they were older than my son, I felt that I could leave them and that they would be OK. I knew they were going to miss us, but I was going to L.A. to work so that I could then bring them to be with us. I know that they will understand that I was just looking for a better life for all of us.

The special moment had finally come: I saw them. At first I didn't know if they were really my parents or just some other human beings. I thought they would look like they did in the pictures I had of them in Mexico, skinny and kind of small, but they looked different. They seemed bigger and well fed, and they both looked a little older. Still, I knew they were my parents. I wondered, if I hug them, will they hug me back?

"*Mis hijas*, how are you both?" my mom said. "Don't be afraid—we're here now. Tell me, how do you two feel?"

"I feel good, and I'm happy to see you again, but I'm also tired," I said.

"Let's go home now so that we can all rest—we'll talk more tomorrow," my mom said.

Then I hugged my mother and my father, and I felt so happy, because I knew that even though it had been a long time since we'd seen each other, they were my parents, and they loved my sister and me.

On the way to the house, we talked about how we felt now that we were together again. My sister and I talked about our lives in Mexico and how much we had both missed them. My mom asked us how my grandparents treated us and if they took good care of us, which they did. At first, talking with them was kind of strange: I was talking to people I hadn't seen for years, but then after a few minutes it felt good to know that here in L.A. I had special people who would take good care of me. I had someone to talk to, someone who would listen to me and give me advice.

I had finally been reunited with my parents, but I was still waiting for one more special moment, which I had been looking forward to the most: I couldn't wait to meet my new brother and sister, who I had never met because they were born in L.A., and I also couldn't wait to see my younger brother Armando again—I hadn't seen him since he was a year old. Because it was nighttime when we arrived home, the children were sleeping, so I only got to watch them as they slept. They looked so innocent. How would they be when they were awake? My brother, whom I hadn't seen for seven years, looked tall and big. Would he like us? Would he ask about our family in Mexico?

I couldn't sleep that night because I was trying to find answers to all of my questions. When I woke up the next morning, I asked my mother where my brother was.

"He went to school; he will be back at two," she said.

I was anxious the whole day until two o'clock finally came and my eight-year-old brother walked through the door. First we stared at each other, then we both smiled and laughed.

"*Hola*," he said.

"*Hola*. You're so big," I replied.

He said, "I grew," and we both laughed again.

"How do you like it here?" he asked me.

"I've just gotten here, but I think I'll like it."

He asked me, "Do you want to learn to speak English? I could help you learn it."

"Thank you," I said, "I would love to learn English, but I don't think I'll like it; I prefer my own language. When you first went to school here, did you like it? Was it difficult for you to learn English?"

"When Mom told me I had to go to school, at first I didn't want to," he answered. "I just wanted to stay home and play. Then our parents told me that if I wanted to be a doctor, a teacher, or any other profession, I had to study—that inspired me, and then I was happy to go. When I met my first teacher, I liked her and the way she explained things to me, the way she helped me learn. If I can learn to speak English, I bet you can learn easily. Now tell me, what it was like for you and Esperanza to live in Mexico? How are our grandparents? Who did you guys play with? What are some of the games you played?"

"The most important thing I want to tell you is that I miss our grandmother, and also our cousins who used to call me 'Mother' because I was the one who took care of them," I replied. "In Mexico we sometimes played with our neighbors, but most of the time we played with our cousins. The thing I liked to do best was play in the field on the other side of the river. We had to cross the *maroma*, a small bridge made out of tree trunks and string, and then we would run to the field. We would get scared when we saw the cows and the *toros* coming toward us. I thought it was funny when Esperanza got scared and ran, but I didn't move because I knew they would go the other way and not hurt us."

"That sounds fun!" said Armando. "I'm sorry, Patricia, but it's getting late, and I need to do my homework. Later I'll introduce you to the neighbors so that we will be able to play with them together—they speak Spanish, so don't worry that you don't speak English. Maybe they also can help you learn English. They can tell you more about Los Angeles and all the things there are to see and do here."

I was relieved to see my brother again and to find him so friendly. I was also so glad to meet my four-year-old sister, and I was surprised at how quickly she became attached to me. My other brother, Mario, was just a year old, and I knew the routine that I had in Mexico wasn't going to change here in L.A.—I was going to take care of him the same way I took care of my little cousins in Mexico. I knew I was going to teach this little piece of new life, my little brother, lessons that would help him in the future. I felt great happiness: my new life in L.A. was starting out so well.

Even though they were worried about the trip up here, I know they are going to be happy again because we are finally together as a family. Before I saw them I was nervous, but now that I've talked to them, I feel that everything is going to be OK. We will never be apart again. Everyone is comfortable together: my other children really like their two big sisters. I am going to put Patricia and Esperanza in school right away; I know they are smart and will easily learn English. They will see the opportunities they have here in L.A. I think they will like Los Angeles and also the neighborhood—they have a house here, they have a family, and I know they are going to have many friends. I just want the best for them. I know they will miss their grandmother, but I think they will get used to it. I will do my best to support them as a mother and help them with whatever I can. I will try to be the best mother for all my children.

I was scared at first at the thought of going to a new school, meeting new people, and learning a new language, but at the same time I was happy to know I was entering a new and exciting world. I did my best to learn English, and I learned really quickly. So far in my life, most of my dreams have come true. I am now working on the one I think is the most important—to become a nurse.

Initially, I came to Los Angeles just to be with my parents, but then I realized that this is a city of opportunities and a city where dreams can come true if you really work to accomplish them. I knew when I came here that my new life was going to be hard, but I know that if I try my best, I'll open the door to the future waiting for me here in L.A.

MY VIOLIN DREAM
MARIA SANCHEZ

At home my life has a slower pace. I can't say that I never rush, because we all do at some point, but my life really starts to rush once I leave my house and walk to the main street. Once I get there, the quiet block that I have just left seems like another world because of the cars, buses, and people rushing all around me. These people don't even look twice at me, and if they stop to say hi, it's some kind of miracle.

At school my life is fast paced, and my lessons pass like a blur; I would hardly remember anything if it weren't for the notes I take in class. In just four months we have to learn everything that we would normally learn in a year. The student population of my school is like that of a small town. People don't care if they push you or if they cut in front of you in the lunch line—if you let yourself be cut in front of, then it will continue to happen to you. Basically, students do not care about anything but getting somewhere first, whether it's to the lunch area or home. They never want to rush to class, however. I can't understand: Why not? I'm the same way, but I go to school to get a good education because I know that will allow me to succeed in life.

Another thing that makes me rush is my love of music. I play the flute in the All-City Band, and being in this band means that that days move very fast and are always full of many pressing things to do: for example, we have to learn and memorize five songs in a small amount of time. I make an exception to all the rushing about where the All-City Band is concerned because music is my passion. It can inspire people to create a more harmonious world.

Sometimes in my third-period chemistry class, I sit at my desk and stare at the periodic table on the wall. Suddenly, I remember old dreams from when I was younger. Some are just childish, like the one about being a mermaid or the one about a talking teacup; at other times in my dreams I was an astronaut, a doctor, a singer, an actress, or a police officer. Recently I dreamt of becoming an FBI agent, and then I taught myself how to play the violin. I felt there was a connection between these two events, but it is a bit difficult to explain it. To me, both of these things are really about creating harmony.

My dream is to play the violin with perfection, but I don't want anyone to teach me—I want to teach myself. I may not play the violin as well as I play the flute, but I do know how to play a song or two. I don't want an instructor to rush me. I want to take my time. I want to learn from my mistakes, because then I will understand myself better. There is something about the violin that makes me think of Renaissance times. Sometimes I wish I had lived back then, because there were a lot of beautiful landscapes with trees and flowers all around. Things moved much more slowly, and it was more serene. When I'm stressed out I like to imagine myself in a place like that, with flowers all around me and the breeze swirling and carrying the sound of my music across the fields, across the city. People would hear my music and enjoy it with me.

In my dream for Los Angeles, people slow down and just enjoy life without rushing anywhere, without wasting precious moments. People value the things that they normally wouldn't, things they take for granted right now. People enjoy the sun, the breeze, the rain. They take a break from their daily routines. They take walks instead of driving their cars, and they stop worrying about if they're going to be late.

What is the point of rushing? Slow down, take the time to learn and enjoy what you like best, and help me make L.A. the place we all dream about.

I DREAM
ROSALINDA ROCHA

I dream of an L.A. with clean streets, where kids won't pick up germs or dangerous items like needles as their mothers tell them, "*No andes agarando eso sino te voy a pegar,*" but they do it anyway. I dream of a place where everyone can pick up after themselves, where we can plant more trees and have nice grass with lots of flowers of every color, red, orange, pink, and purple. It looks nicer, and you can actually breathe clean air instead of all the smog and that horrible smell of fish mixed with diapers and spoiled food. (Have you seen the TV commercial that says that the worst thing is having your house smell like fish and flowers?)

I dream of an L.A. with less violence, so we won't be afraid to play outside. Or fear being run over by a drunk driver. Or worry about people offering you drugs on almost every corner; they mostly come out at night, like wolves just waiting for their next victim. I dream of more shelters so there aren't so many homeless people on the street bugging you and saying offensive things like, "*Oye mamasita, a donde vas tan apurada,*" or whistling or sending you kisses—things that you don't like or that make you uncomfortable.

I dream of an L.A. with more schools, so every student can have a better learning environment, where there are not thirty-two kids in a small classroom with no air-conditioning and just one teacher who can't help them graduate because they don't get the attention they need. The majority of the students are Latinos who are not graduating, and people are saying, "Hey, just drop out. It's not like you're going to be anything in life." Because of that—and many reasons more—their self-esteem goes down, and they are left thinking that the only thing they can do in this world is flip burgers and repeat the phrase, "Do you want ketchup with that?"

I dream of an L.A. with more after-school programs like sports or Teens Helping Teens, so fewer kids will fall into drugs or gangs because they think that it's the only way out or that it makes them cool. I dream of more opportunities for undocumented people to get better jobs so they won't have to suffer in fields, sweating, not getting enough water and fainting, or even dying.

I dream of an L.A. in which we can provide a good environment for ourselves, for our children, and for future generations, an L.A. in which you can say, "I did something to make a difference in this beautiful city."

A WAY TO DREAM
KRISTOPHER ESCAJEDA

Eyes get heavy
Body becomes free
Prepare yourself
For the city dream

Never been to a place like this before
My mind is confused, it opens new doors
Cannot tell from what is real
Heart adjusting to gain back feel

Walking in the street
Competing with cars
Hearing footsteps on the pavement
As the streetlights swing from the bars

Cluttered by a cloud
Of everyone's thoughts
Can't control this environment
So I pause and thought

Why is everyone in a rush?
Take your time people
Like a painter using his brush

The sounds of the city
Should sound so fair
Using its pounding noise
To paint colors in the air

Being divided by the wall of the city
A homeless man understands my pity

Being judged and also labeled
I lay examples on the table

A man was walking down the street
With no money in his pocket
It was taken by a tall thin man
Thinking that stealing
Is his only helping hand

Many people think
That the city is nothing less than
A landfill of corrupted minds
And no one to caress

You must know we're a large family
Living life with no trust
In this community

We are all equal
But express things our own way
That's what makes us unique
Every single day

As this dream comes to an end
I find myself back in my bed
Knowing what I know now
I understand the troubles that I found

NAKED EYES
CRISTINA CORREA

Close your eyes follow the dark blue sea
The moon will appear on the true right
The sun and stars will appear on the left
Future lies beneath the stars, as naked eyes can't see
But when they fall into my long deep spell
The stars show the truth about life.

There is a man who names his child Los Angeles.
And his eyes show the life and names of those who died.
My child has gone to a place, the land of love.
He whispers tears in my ear and there appears a sad, lonely girl.
He tries to speak a word of fear and I show him the path to the stars
And he opens his mind to truth.

Now he fears a threat to his long-lost love.
Roses fall from the sky to show the tears he cried.
My heart breaks and I open my eyes and see a man with a smile.
He points and I go to that place and the land is sweet.
My eyes widen. People are gone.

I see a woman laughing and she looks at me and says,
"Hello, my pretty child. Don't be scared.
Just close your eyes and follow me to that land.
You will see a man walking the road and
A woman dancing on the moon with her children
And she will open your mind and you will see her eyes filled with love."

She smiles and calls me to fill dreams for the weaker ones.

MY BROWN EYES
ALEXANDER AMADOR

I was born in Boyle Heights and grew up in the barrio of the Eighth Street Locos 13 gang. The 'hood is cool; I love my neighborhood. I love it so much that sometimes I feel that I should be part of it, but something just holds me back: my *Jefita*, the one who cares, the one who will give up her life for mine. She didn't have it easy. *Mi Jefita*, Macrina N., doesn't even know how to read or write, not even her own name.

It's pretty messed up how many of us Mexicans come to the United States to get a better chance in life, but it all just seems to go wrong. We get hooked on drugs or just gang bang. Homie, this isn't the life for us—there's more to life, *ese*. What about graduating from high school? What about having a job, a career, something to be proud of? Gang wars are pretty stupid once you think about it: they kill our own *raza,* and for what? For nothing! Us "Browns" should be united—you know, just like Martin Luther King Jr. said, "I have a dream . . .," and my dream is for all Mexicans to shake hands and say, "*Orale.*"

Homies from my 'hood are like family. They tell me what to do and what not to do. Eighth Street is more like a gang: when they're united they stand, but divided they fall. "Lil Smiley" and "Vamps," they stay up night and day *controlando las calles de la ocho.* Their saying to other *lames* is "If you can't hang, don't bang with the Eighth Street Gang!" They are good homies, though; they helped me through good times and bad. When I didn't have *feria,* they would try to help me out; they would've taken me in their *cantón* to eat yesterday's *pozole.* Even though they gang banged, I knew they really cared for a little youngster like me. When I was in a bad situation, they would tell me that they would handle it. They told me to keep my head in school because it didn't have to be this way, I could reach for more. My homies have those bad times, too, but we're there for each other. No one gets left behind: "You need $1.07 for a Big Mac? Don't trip . . . here, homie." It's just like that oldie jam says, "Look over your shoulder, you'll find me."

Sometimes I look at my mom and I just can't believe what she's been through. No dad, but that's nothing unusual. My brother got sent away on the day before Halloween for violating his probation. My mom cried every morning, and all the tears she cried were tears of caring, the tears of a loving mother. My brother had two sides; he had his drug troubles, but he was also that guy who really helped her out. Even though he didn't have a job, his money came from what he loved the most, the weed. My mom did not want to accept his money, but my brother would insist, telling her that he had a "little job." He would read the papers that came in the mail and translate them for her. Whatever she asked, he would do— he had so much respect for her.

It's not hard to be a good son and still kick it with the homeboys. Our mothers deserve more than just payment of rent or money to buy some groceries for the *familia*—they should receive love and respect, because that's what family is all about. I don't understand why we don't listen to our mothers. My mom tells me reality, but I turn my back on it. I guess it's just part of life and growing up.

Ever since my brother was arrested, I've been the one who translates for my mother. Right after school I go straight home and clean up the mess that my little brother and my little sister have made. I take the meat out of the freezer and put it in a pot full of hot water so that by the time my mom comes home, she doesn't have so many things to worry about, like: "What is there to cook? All the food is frozen? The house is a mess!" I don't like seeing her upset, so I try to help her out; it's not much, but I try. I realize that my brother's job wasn't as simple as I thought.

I see a new reality now: my *carnal*, my brother, is going to college over by Rancho San Antonio, working at some place called Jamba Juice, talking about how he wants to be someone in life, and I think that's really *firme*; the first person in our *familia* wanting to succeed. I just hope he does so that I can believe in miracles. He still insists on giving my mom some money, and I know he really cares. He tells me that he doesn't want to come back home because he knows it's all going to come back to him. He tells my mom to move away from the projects, but you know, Homes, there isn't any other place like home.

WALKING, TALKING, AND THINKING
ARNOLD PRIETO

It's 7:30 AM and I just walked into my middle school cafeteria. As I drag myself in, my legs can't stop shaking, my fists are in a ball, and the sweat on my forehead drops like the morning's dew. "Where is he at? Damn, what's taking him so long to get here?" I ask myself in a state of panic. The morning is still not clear. The sun is still down; kids keep coming into school as they do every day of the week.

The blue shorts of my uniform do not keep out much of the coldness in the foggy air. Numerous students surround me. "You ain't gonna beat up nobody, cuz," one of them says. And as soon as my brain soaks in those words, Eric Estrada (not *the* Erik Estrada; this Eric Estrada—unlike the actor—is a puny fourteen-year-old Salvadoran) pops out like a gopher from his hole. So the chase begins. I see my friends chasing Eric around the school grounds. They're bigger and faster then me. They are fourteen- and fifteen-year-olds, and meaner than me. For a moment I lose sight of them, but as soon as I see them cross the street away from school and the watching crowd, I know they have Eric down on the ground.

"Why did you do it? Who's behind all of this?" One of the LAPD police officers questions me. "Man, I don't know . . . I don't know," I say. Oh, but I do know. My knees are now wobbly, and my heart hammers my body. After I calm down, I explain my story to the officers.

It all started on a hot sticky afternoon on campus right next to the boy's gym as I stood close to my friend Felipe, your typical eighth-grade troublemaker. Felipe fought every day and didn't have a care in the world about what happened to him—he was the kind of kid who worried about things the next day and did not worry about the present. He couldn't stop himself from talking smack to Eric. I'm not sure what they were arguing about—I wasn't paying much attention—but it wasn't the first time they had exchanged words in an angry manner. The bell rang for third period, and they reacted as if they were in a boxing ring. Felipe threw a right cross onto Eric's ear. "Ooohhhhhh," the crowd cheered. Administrators came around the corner, and Felipe told me, "Hey foo', I'll see ya at home, I'm ditching and going home. I don't want to get suspended." Felipe and I had been neighbors since I was six years old, and he was my best friend. I understood his situation and gave him a nod. He turned around, jumped the fence, and headed home.

As I walked home, passing by El Pollo Loco and Taco Bell and crossing the street away from the Bank of America, I saw Eric walking in my direction and looking at me with this evil look that you get when you can't release the pressure inside yourself. I was walking with my "friend" Antonio and talking to him about the fight between Felipe and Eric. I'm walking, talking, and thinking calmly, not knowing what was about to happen two more steps beyond the sidewalk.

As I stepped off the broken gray sidewalk on the main street, I saw Eric's eye look at me dead on, and then I felt a hard hit. I had to react. Eric punched my head with lots of anger, the same anger Felipe had for him. I threw as many punches as I could, but I was no match for an eighth-grader. We stopped for a brief second and I heard screaming on the buses, cars beeping, people on the street telling us to keep on fighting—"Stop! Get him, Arnold!"—and then I hear Antonio say, "Take out your shank!" I was confused about the words coming out of his mouth— I didn't have any kind of weapon on me. Eric didn't think twice before he picked up an object that looked to me like a baseball bat, but it was only a wooden stick. I told Eric, "I don't have a shank. Drop it." And as soon I said that, there was a moment of stillness.

I stood up and walked away with my tail between my legs. I cried all the way home; I had little girl tears sliding down my cheeks. They were tears of madness, of disappointment, and hate. I should have hurt him until he cried, but I was small and not a real good fighter, so I couldn't leave as many marks as he left upon me.

I got home after the worst, longest thirty minutes of my life. Damn, I had to hold in the pain and keep my secret from my mom, but not from my friends—oh no, not them; I had to tell them every single detail to get my sweet revenge. My friends gathered and we made plans about what we had to do. We never thought about the consequences we would have to deal with.

We decided to leave early in the morning, find Eric, and as soon as we captured him, take him down without any regrets. A friend's mom dropped us off at school, and we all got out of the car with strong nerves. We lifted our heads and walked in, searching for Eric on the school grounds. We found him eventually, and now I've found myself stuck here in handcuffs and giving my version of what happened.

The officer told me that what we decided was a bad thing to do, that we should've told an administrator and everything could have been avoided. (Grown-ups always say that approach works, but it never does—it just causes more drama and fights.) The officer let me and my friends go after giving us each two tickets, one for truancy and one for fighting; I took care of the tickets through anger management classes.

Well, things didn't end there. My mom, so careful and so worried, decided to transfer me from that school so she wouldn't have to worry about any other serious problems. So I decided to go to my cousin's school in East Los Angeles—I had to travel miles and across three different cities just to escape the difficulties that I had encountered in South Central. There, during my seventh-grade year, I had to accustom myself to a new society and atmosphere. The people in my new school were different and all had faces I had never seen before, but I soon found myself making friends and going on with my life. Eighth grade came, and it was one of the most magnificent years of my school life. My grades were good, and the friction with the kids wasn't so hard on me. Here I could be who I wanted to be and do almost everything without the fear of assault or endangerment to myself.

Once I cut my hair and got a different look, people started to like me more, and I really enjoyed that. I was soon one of the cool, popular kids in school; I never would have expected that at my old school. I was nominated as the most unique kid in school—and I actually won the position and became even more popular. By this point I had my Mohawk, hair sticking up in spikes. I used to spike it up with beeswax, and it lasted only about half a day; after PE during fourth period, with all the running and exercising, it fell down a lot. I also had a unique way of making my middle-school uniform look more radical.

Life wasn't much better at first, but it got better over the years. I got interested in music and musicians like Rage Against the Machine and Sublime, who encouraged me to listen and inspired me to make some music of my own. That's when I decided to get a guitar and give it a try. I told my sweet, hard-working parents that I really wanted a guitar for Christmas and that I would learn how to play it very well. My musical life didn't change much at first because I could only practice alone. I didn't know any other musicians to practice or play with.

One day I was skateboarding with my friend Miguel, and when we sat down to take a break, we started to talk about where to skate on Saturday. One thing led to another, the subject changed, and we started to talk about music. I mentioned that I had a guitar. Miguel told me, "I have drums at my house, and it would be cool if we tried to make songs together and practice." I agreed, and my first band was formed. At first we only covered songs—or at least we thought we did, because we weren't very good at the time; we were beginners and could only play beats.

We got better over the years and began to think about what to name the band. We came up with Avoid, but that didn't last long. We came up with S.C. Punx but then found out that was a crew, so we had to change it one more time. I finally thought about a good one relating to what we were and what my mother called us a lot: Los Callejeros, "street brats," because we were out all day and night. That name stuck to us. After several months my friend and I stopped talking because we had a big fight. We were making a music video and were supposed to end the video fighting. The fake fight ended up being a real one, and we didn't talk for a long time afterwards. Miguel went his own way, and I decided to find new band members. That's when Felipe came back in the picture. Felipe had lots of interest in music as well and has always had a desire to play with my band. He joined in, along with my other friend from middle school, George. Finally we had a full three-man band.

Music for me was just like candy—sweet and tasty. I started to explore a lot, listening to different styles of music. It was a coincidence that one day in the tenth grade I met Angel in Spanish class. Angel is a funny guy, slim, dark, and easy to get along with. He told me that he had a ska band named Drunk Skunks (which was later changed to Ultima Caida), and from the way he described the band, they sounded pretty good. He said, "We are just starting to play out but already have songs done to play at gigs." I never heard of any genre named ska—I was mostly into punk music—so Angel invited me to his house, where they practiced in the basement. I ducked down into the crowded, dark, cozy room and what I heard was good, and catchy, too. I really liked them.

After time passed and I had been to some of their gigs, they told me they were in need of a *timbalero*. I told my mom; she had heard Angel's band, and she liked them as well. She told me that I should join them and that she would buy me those timbales. Soon enough I found myself in Sam Ash's music store in search of my own timbales.

I got my timbales in October, just two weeks before the first public show I ever played—I had roughly that much time to practice along with the band's demo. At home in my own little world, I practiced until my parents got disturbed and asked me to stop. I only knew the most basic fundamentals about playing timbales, but that was enough for me to play my first gig. These were some of the most exciting weeks of my life as I asked everyone I knew to go see me play and support my band. The days flew by, and I soon found myself a day away from playing at a show in East Los Angeles at La Terraza Jamay. When we got to the place, butterflies were flying around in my stomach because I had the heebie-jeebies. We finally played, and the crowd cheered; they asked for an encore but we had to get off the stage to let the other bands play. My first show, my first performance—unbelievable.

Soon after, we played lots of shows around East Los Angeles and South Central, at high schools like Garfield and Roosevelt. Then we played in Hollywood, at the Key Club. I realized that the decisions that I had made were outstanding: I had found a band that I really liked, and here I was in Ultima Caida, playing a big venue. Looking back at my old life and my karma, I never would have imagined myself playing with an actual band in a famous location.

L.A. is made up of lots of wonderful people and environments that show the difference in people's taste. There are lots of different places in L.A. where one can go and find new experiences, people, and activities. I found music.

Since that fight with Eric, I have not fought again. Music hasn't brought any troubles to my life, only lots of hard thinking and composing. I have had enemies in life, but none like Eric; most of my enemies are fictional. One good thing about music: when it hits you, you feel no pain.

When I was thirteen years old, I thought I was going to be a pro skater. If life hadn't taken a different turn, I would have continued skating with all of my friends, going to the extremes, breaking into skate parks or going onto private property just to improve our moves and tricks so that one day a skate shop or company would sponsor us and make us pro skaters. However, to my surprise, I found myself in a whole different picture . . .

A CAR: A MUST-HAVE FOR TEENS IN L.A.
ALEJANDRO ROSALES

"Dream" is a word that people think about and express in different ways. My type of dream is my future job, home, and family, and many other things I would like to have. All that is ahead of me, but right now my dream is a car—so many bus rides are driving me nuts. I need a car.

I especially need a car in this wonderful city called Los Angeles, where the only sort of good transportation is a car. But I don't want one of those cheap Oldsmobiles; I want something nice. This is the turning point for me. A car is the first thing I need to start reaching for my dreams. Think about it: it could take me to school earlier, so I don't miss any lectures, and I could get my homework done earlier, which leads to better grades, and that means more free time, which leads to getting a job, and I'd have the car that could take me to the job. A car is the first step.

I wake up at 5:30 AM in the morning and fall back to sleep hoping no one will notice and leave me there. Thirty minutes later I get a wake-up call, and slowly, like a lifeless body, I get up and try to find my towel, which migrated overnight from hanging on the door to the bottom of my closet.

After the shower, it's like a lightning bolt hit me. I get my energy and get dressed in a hurry because I'm always running late. My mom just won't stop telling me that if I get to school late one more time she won't give me money for the bus. When I get out the door it's like I'm walking with all the calm in the world to the bus stop.

Waiting for the bus is like déjà vu. It's an endless cycle, you stand there for ten minutes and wait to see if that midget bus is going to stop or not. I see the same faces waiting for the bus the whole year round. It's like family: some you hate, some you love, and some, you realize, you don't know at all. The bus ride to school is the worst feature of a regular school day. If you're lucky, you get a seat, but most of the time you're crammed in and you can't move because you have a person on every side. It feels like you can't breathe. The bus' capacity is about thirty to thirty-five, but on a regular school day it's about sixty people jammed shoulder to shoulder, packed in.

While I'm on the bus during the twenty minutes it takes to get to school, I look over my shoulder and see all the cars zoom by, comparing them one by one. I see cars I would have and cars I wouldn't even show my face in. After watching cars for a few minutes, my mind wanders off to the best joyride I ever had.

A joyride is best experienced at 2 or 3 AM in the morning. Once when I went on vacation to Sahuayo, Mexico, I was in my cousin's ferocious 2004 F-150 truck, fixed up with a monster sound system so loud the bass rumbles through your chest: fifteen-inch woofers, six-inch mid- speakers, and four tweeters. We cruised all over the city, blasting Los Originales de San Juan, making car alarms blare. Heads turned, people stared, and we were known as the two guys with the greatest car in town.

But now I'm here on the bus, drowsy, nauseated, worried my breakfast burrito is going to make a reappearance onto someone's lap.

The only thing worse than taking the bus in the morning is taking it at night. Last month I was invited to my friend's *quinciñera*. Because neither my mom nor I have a car, I had to ask my friend Vero to ask her parents to drive me—how embarrassing. I thought it was going to be boring and I was only going to stay two hours, but *au contraire*, the party was great, and it was suddenly 11:25 PM—and I had to take the 11:30 bus home.

By 11:25, I was waiting for the bus. I waited an hour at a stop behind a shopping center. It was lonely; I was the only person waiting. I was just standing there, and out of nowhere a Ford Expedition stops and the passengers start calling me. I look. There are three bald guys, and living in East L.A. you know that means—gang members. I think, "Do I really look like a rival gang member?"

While I'm thinking that, they keep calling to me, but out of nowhere a girl's voice inside the car keeps saying, "Forget it. Leave."

Luckily they did, and my body felt about ten pounds lighter. The bus took another thirty minutes to arrive after that ordeal. When the bus came, I said some gibberish while getting on, and the bus driver looked at me funny. I said, "Sorry," and took a seat.

I was so relieved to get home safely. As I fell asleep, I said to myself, "That's the last time I'm ever taking the bus at midnight."

So I'm still thinking: How many more situations do I have to go through for my mom to notice that the bus is a dangerous place? Do I have to lose a leg, or what? If I had a car, none of these horrendous things would happen. Mom, if you're reading this, this is your only son, who loves and cares for you. If I got a car, you wouldn't need to worry about me coming home late, or worse. Doesn't that sound heartwarming?

So that's my thought about my dreams here in L.A. Have you thought about yours? You don't need to be in L.A., but wherever you live, . . . think about it and get back to me.

BUS BUDDIES
LADY SEPULVEDA

Where is Liz?
                Waiting, waiting, and waiting for the bus
                        [oh no! late again?]
Hey, finally, it's coming, yeah, oh never mind, it's the 362, or 65, or
just Not In Service
                [now I'm definitely late]
                I see it coming from way far away, wonder,
                                    [can I make it on time?]

It's coming! It's coming! It's the one. I get excited.
                        [not getting detention like last time]
Before I get on I see that it's crowded, barely enough room to walk through.
[I wonder how I'll get out]
                Looking for my weekly pass,
                        [oh my god did I lose it again?]
        Take out the three dollars to buy my pass.
                Now I can't buy *diablito,* that's not fair.
                        The three stubborn dollars refuse to go in.
[is everyone looking at me?]
                        The more I push them, the less that they'll go in.
                        People are waiting in back of me.
        The money disappears and I walk up the aisle looking for a seat.
The bus driver floors it
                        [I almost fall]
                I actually push a kid and step on an old man,
        [I feel so bad]
                        Can only say "sorry" and keep on looking for a seat.
I look and look for a seat and try not to fall or trip.
                        A long way ahead,
                It's getting very crowded
                        Now I will have to push to get out.

There are just way too many people it reminds me of a can of sardines
[something about the small space and too many people in it]
 I stop for a moment and wonder, where are all of these people going?

                         I see and hear Spanish everywhere.
Halfway along the first part of the ride,
                         I see the orange buildings, the projects.
   [here we go, you thought it was crowded, now it is two times worse]
The bus makes a stop 1, 2, 3 . . . 20 people get on, damn, that's a lot.
   The bus is now so full that I wonder if he is going to stop
      at the next stop.
Actually I don't think that we can fit anybody else in.
                     I can smell the French fries of the "M" we are near.
   The bus is turning, I start to get up.
   I am wondering whether to get out through the front or the back.
                                   Back is closer, I guess.
                               Touch, touch, touch.
               It is hard to get out,
      I have to say excuse me, excuse me, *con permiso*, a lot of times
[but when that does not work pushing will do it]
               I think to myself, hey, what's up with that,
[before I get off through the back, people are pushing to get on]
                  I think in my head, This is not the front!
                  I finally make it off.

I hear my stomach rumbling,
      What's the first thing that I see? Winchell's Donuts staring at me.
               I am now definitely hungry, mmm, mmm
      I can taste the sweet donuts and the delicious coffee.
                  Walk to the crosswalk.
               Push, push, and push the button,
                  Until I see the green light
So I cross the street.
         Went to wait for the next bus, at the bus stop, yeah, yeah, yeah
There are a lot of people; hopefully it will come by fast.
I don't care whether it is 251 or 252, they'll take me to the same place.
      I am thrilled
                  [no detention today]
                         I start smiling.

My manners go bye-bye
I start to walk towards the bus, pushing small, young, and even old.
I know it is wrong, but that does not stop me.
I do what I have to do to get inside.
It's 7:07, if this thing hurries I'll make it.
We pass through the tunnel of darkness, where homeless lie.
It gives me a weird feeling,
It is actually the only place throughout the ride when I want the bus to
go superfast.
After that the freeway exit comes by.
Then *se empiezan a percinar.*
We pass the church and I see a large statue of Jesus.
{it calms me down}
Look to the back of the bus, there is a seat.
But that's not all that I see.
I see perfection, "my dream guy," looking towards me.
He is not too tall, or too short, just like me.
He has what I like to call sexy hair, just right.
He looks Latino to me, and when he smiles it's better than chocolate
chip ice cream.
So I have a plan,
In order to get to the back, I have to pass next to him, and we
will touch.
Pass next to my dream guy, wow, he is so hot.
He is so hot that I can't be next to him;
{I get those butterflies}
Then he passes by and our hands rub against each other,
I want to stay like that forever.
So he says that he is sorry, he thought he had pushed me.
I just smile and say it is OK.
I walk towards the empty seat and sit down.
I smile as I think back on it.
But then he pulls the cord and out the door he goes,
I'll probably never see him again.
Sad, but I still have a magical moment to share.
I'll will tell Dalia and Liz some other day.
Then "Stop Requested" for me,
I stumble off.
And the bus goes on.

BLACK SHEEP?
VIRIDIANA BERNAL

L.A. is not the black sheep of California
As the movies seem to draw it in people's heads . . .
Needing a place to point and shoot at people—BANG!
The movies encourage gangs to multiply throughout L.A.
Like scattering ants searching for food at the beginning of winter . . .

Hearing gunshots through the windows and the flashing colors in the
shadows. The sirens. AGAIN . . .

L.A.'s the place where you don't sleep 'cause of the blinding light,
sirens and noise.
While mothers' sons die, dads' brothers die, and friends die, life
moves on.
Like time. There is nothing anyone can do to stop it or return to the past.

No God, no love, no good memories . . . nothing.
Not even memories of them laughing . . . nothing can bring them back.
It burns you from the inside like an inferno,
Feeling helpless, knowing that their life will end someday
Like different-colored leaves falling from a tree on an autumn day.
No wind can place it back to its proper branch, no nourishment can
revive it.

But people who live here have different experiences of L.A.

It has great sushi that makes your mouth water with just one taste,
Probably how a hungry fish feels right before taking the bait.

Downtown, all the different people walking back and forth.
You enjoy the rhythm of their footsteps almost making a beat.
Time seems to fly with each step, the people make it to their destinations.

If you look at the windows of the skyscrapers, you can see yourself in
a different time . . .

Looking up you can see another dimension.
Passing store after store and entering another era . . . Chinatown.
A fantastic place with delicious food and perfect anime!
Wise older Chinese people . . . wishing you could learn their life.
You could even forget you are still in L.A.

Many parents believe that their children are like banks: "*Banco
sin fondos* . . ."
You have to give to the bank, but there's no guaranteed return.
Your parents sacrifice their hands for you, so do something
worthwhile . . .
Explore.

L.A. streets are best seen through the windows of the buses.
From Eighth Street to school, there's a bus at the corner.
From Whittier Street to Downtown, there's a bus at the corner.
And to anywhere else you may want to discover,
There will eventually be a bus at the corner.

From the bus windows you can see beautiful murals,
Waiting to be seen by unfamiliar eyes . . .
Not just primary colors, but all the colors in the rainbow, shown to
Express different cultures, ideas for the future and from the past.

You can walk to school and admire the murals in the streets . . .
Expressing the colors of the Mexican culture and shouting out to be seen
By the rest of the world.

You may look at the creations with curiosity,
Even find a place in your heart that you never knew you had.
It might surprise you to learn a new perspective on who you really are.

Looking and stopping and thinking and imagining and then . . .
DREAMING.

The eye of the world watches L.A.

THE GOOD IN EVERYTHING
JENNIFER GUERRA

A new life, a new place: these were the things that one girl dreamed about. Her name was Hope, and she lived in East L.A. with her parents. Like any girl, Hope went to school, but she also had a part-time job in a small store. She didn't get paid a lot, but some of what she made she gave to her parents, and the rest she would just put away. Her dream was to save enough money to move far away—she was tired of gunshots at night when she was trying to sleep. Hearing shots was such a common occurrence for her that she no longer paid attention. She was not terribly surprised when she heard about accidents or death, but she never thought that something like that would happen to her.

Mrs. Honey, the owner of the store where Hope worked, was always elegant and well dressed. She told Hope about her many travels to different places, and how she'd gotten her education in Europe. "Everyone is so educated in Europe—it's nothing like here," she told Hope. Since that conversation, Hope had made a promise to herself: she would find the perfect place for herself, a place where she would be happy.

Hope had a best friend named Grace. She had met Grace at work, and they had become best friends. Since Grace had a car, she would often give Hope a ride home. The two girls did everything together.

It was 8 PM, and you could clearly see the bright stars in the dark sky. Hope and Grace had just finished their shift and were driving home. All of a sudden, they heard the sound of police sirens, so Grace pulled over. The cops were chasing someone who was fleeing in a car, and as they turned the corner, a police car hit Grace's car, spinning it into the middle of the intersection. Hope was hurt but still alive, and she turned to her friend. Grace was bleeding—her head had hit the windshield.

"Grace! Are you all right? Talk to me," said Hope, shaking.

Grace opened her eyes, "I don't fe . . . eel . . ." she said, coughing up blood.

"Grace!"

"I . . . I don't want to . . . ," said Grace, and then she closed her eyes.

One police car continued chasing the speeding car, but the other stopped. The cops helped Hope out of the car, and they also pulled Grace's body onto the pavement. Hope was up on her feet, watching a cop cover Grace.

"Are you all right?" the policeman asked.

She only said one thing—"I want to go home"—and then stayed quite still, looking at her friend's dead body.

When the policemen asked her where she lived, Hope didn't answer, but her ID, with her address printed on it, was in her backpack. One cop guided her into his car and drove her home.

When Hope's parents opened the door and saw her standing there with a cop, their faces were filled with horror, as if they had seen a ghost. As the policeman explained what had happened, Hope's mother and father stood with their mouths open; they could barely believe what they were hearing, but they were very relieved to have their daughter home alive. It was not until later that Hope found out that the speeding car had been driven by a drunk driver.

As the cop spoke, Hope ran to her room and lay on her bed, a pillow to her face, and cried. She didn't even bother to turn on the lights. Later, her mother knocked on the door and softly asked, "Sweetie, are you all right? Can I help?"

"Leave her alone," said Hope's father with a calm voice, but his face showed concern.

It took Hope five days to calm herself enough to stop crying all the time. She would hardly eat a thing and she didn't go to school—she didn't even leave her room. Finally, her mother knocked and entered her bedroom, carrying a tray with food; it was so dark that she could hardly see. The curtains covered the window so little light penetrated the room, but she was able to make out her daughter's puffy red eyes.

"How are you feeling? A little better?" said her mother with such a sweet voice that it only made Hope want to cry some more.

"If only she hadn't stopped, if only she'd had her seat belt on, if only she hadn't driven me home, if only she didn't live here, if only . . . " Tears rolled down Hope's cheeks. Her mother put the tray on top of the dresser and hugged her daughter, comforting her. It was the first time she had heard her daughter say anything since the day of the accident.

Seven days passed after Grace's death. On the day of Grace's funeral,

Hope got up, took a shower, and dressed all in black. Her parents were also dressed in black. Hope didn't want to go—she didn't want to see all the suffering—but she knew she had to. It was her best friend who had died. She had to go and pay her respects.

They got into the car and headed to the church. Hope looked out the window and saw her neighborhood. She saw some kids tagging on the wall of a bakery as people passed by, pretending they didn't see anything. She saw cops talking to a couple of boys, and once in a while she would hear an ambulance.

Graffiti, fights, death, suffering—is this all that awaits me here? she wondered.

When they arrived at the church, Hope saw Grace's mother, who was crying. Hope didn't know what to say, except that she was sorry.

"It's not your fault, Hope," Grace's mom said, and then she turned to face Hope's parents. Hope could not help but feel that Grace's family did blame her for what happened and that they was right to blame her. She felt guilty inside.

Hope wandered off; she was looking for a chair to sit in when she saw Brian, Grace's brother. He was twenty years old (she was seventeen). She remembered how she and Grace would make fun of him. Grace said her parents named him Brian because it was so close to "brain," because he had a big head when he was born. And she had said that they named her Grace because she was always so sweet and made no fuss.

He didn't have a big head now—he had grown into his body. In a way, he was like Hope's older brother too. When she would go to Grace's house and he was there, they had so much fun. He acted like a jerk sometimes, but he was a great listener. He looked so unlike Grace that you could hardly believe they were brother and sister. Grace had black curly hair, light brown eyes, and her skin was of a tan color just like Hope's, but Brian had light brown hair and eyes, and his skin was much lighter.

Hope thought about talking to him but decided not to because she had no idea what to say; she just wanted to be alone. She found a chair near the door and sat down. The entire funeral lasted about four hours, and to Hope it felt like forever. Finally, her dad walked up to her and said, "It's time for us to be on our way." Hope stood up and followed without saying a word.

The next day she stood in her room trying to figure out what she would do now. "I know that I will never go back to the store, that is for sure," she said to herself.

She heard a knock on the front door. She used to always run to answer it, hoping that it was Grace, but now she really didn't care who it was. A few minutes later, her mother came to her bedroom door.

"Grace's brother is here to see you; he said he wants to talk to you," she said.

"Me?"

"Yes, he's waiting in the living room. Now don't be rude, go receive him," her mother said as she turned away.

Hope slowly walked toward the living room. She felt happy as a baby bird when it sees its parents returning after a long hunt, but she was afraid that Brian was going to show her or tell her something she didn't want to know.

Brian stood by the small brown sofa. He was dressed in black just as Hope was.

"Hi," she said, so softly that Brian could hardly hear her say it.

"Hey, how have you been?"

Hope shrugged her shoulders.

"Well, I thought that maybe we could talk," he said.

Still Hope said nothing, but she nodded her head. She didn't know why she could not talk to him; when she used to go to Grace's house he'd seemed like her brother, but now she felt as if he were a stranger.

Brian was not comfortable either, especially with Hope's mother eyeing them from the kitchen; he knew he couldn't really talk to Hope with her watching.

"Do you want to take a walk?" he asked.

Hope looked at her mother. She nodded and said, "It's 6:30; be back by 9."

Outside, they walked along in silence until Brian finally spoke. "Hope, what do you plan to do now?"

She stopped in her tracks. "I don't know, but now more then ever I feel that there is nothing here for me. I just want to forget this; I don't want to keep remembering Grace's face as she died . . ." Tears were rolling down her cheeks.

Brian went to her and put his arms around her and hugged her close—and she didn't back away. When Hope's tears stopped, Brian let her go. Her words told him that what Grace had once told him was true: she had said that Hope was too negative, that she could not see the beauty around her.

"Let's go to the park," he said.

In a whisper, she said, "OK."

As they reached the main park building where the stars were the brightest, Brian suddenly asked her something very strange. "What do you see?"

"Is this a trick question?"

"No, no—just tell me what you see," he said.

"OK. Well . . . I see tagging, a building in bad condition, some troublemakers." There were kids near the door.

"I thought you might say that, but have you ever been on the other side of that door?"

Hope blushed and said, "No, I usually get out of work at eight, so it's too dark to go in there."

"Well, come on—it's only 7:30," Brian said, walking towards the building with his hands in his pockets.

Hope didn't move. Brian stopped and turned, nodding his head forward, and Hope followed him. He stopped and talked to the two kids that Hope had said were troublemakers. One was taller then the other, with long black hair in a ponytail. The smaller boy had short, black, spiky hair.

"Hi, Brian. So you're going to help us out on Monday?" said the small one.

"Yeah," Brian answered.

"Brian, tomorrow is Saturday, painting day . . . are you coming?" asked the other boy.

"Yes . . . oh." He turned to Hope and introduced her to the kids. "This is Zack, he's fifteen, and Jack, he's twelve; they're brothers. Jack comes here every Monday to play basketball, and Zack is painting a mural on one of the walls by the quad. Actually, a lot of people are coming to help paint."

"I didn't know that," she said.

Brian started walking. "Yeah . . . Well, see you later, you guys . . . come on, Hope, take a look on the other side of the building."

She was surprised by what she saw. It was nothing like what she imagined. Most of the walls featured some type of mural. Some featured little kids with farm animals, cows and some chickens. Other murals were more artistic, with pictures of people and objects.

Hope saw rooms, and they were not empty: they were full of kids. There were children from five to ten years old, as well as some who looked to her to be from twelve to about eighteen. The smallest of the kids in the park were in the gym—they were wearing white and were kicking each

other, practicing karate. Some of the older kids, mostly girls, were dancing hip hop.

"Wow, I didn't know about all of this," said Hope as she looked
around.

"Yeah, well, you never came in. They have dance classes here, karate,
basketball, and even crafts. Look, we said we would be back by 9, but I
wanted to talk to you about one more thing," said Brian as they walked
back the way they came. Zack and Jack had gone home. "Hope, I have to
come and help on Saturday. Do you want to come too?"

"Sure," she said, still astonished. "So what did you want to talk to me
about?"

They were again outside the quad.

"You know how you said you saw tagging—why do you think people do that?" Brian asked.

"Well . . . um . . . I guess because they think it's cool," she answered.

Brian responded, "Really? I don't think so. I think they just want to
show that they exist—they want to be noticed."

Hope looked at Brian's face as he looked at the wall. She knew he was
serious and that maybe he was right.

Brian walked Hope back home. When they reached her front door, he
said, "I'm going to the park at 10 AM Want me to come for you?"

"Sure," she said, and went inside.

Hope went to the park with Brian and helped with the mural. At first
it had no shape, but at the end of the day it was halfway done. You could
see the shapes of kids playing and adults talking; it looked like a big party.
Over the next few weeks she spent more time with Brian at the park, and
she was feeling a lot happier. She started to see another side of what she had
thought was bad, like the tagging. She was also getting to know Brian better. He would pick her up after school and they would head to the park. As
they worked with different groups of kids, she would turn to look at Brian,
and he would also turn to stare at her. Sometimes, if he stared for too long,
the kids he was playing basketball with would hit him with the ball.

One night Hope was walking to the park by herself; Brian had to run
an errand, but he was going to meet her there. A block away from the
park, she saw two guys coming towards her. She didn't know why, but seeing them gave her goose bumps, and the hair on the back of her neck stood
up. She was not sure what to do at first, but she then decided that it was
just her imagination. She convinced herself that there was nothing wrong,
and she kept walking.

She took hold of her purse tightly and walked past them. She thought she was fine, but then she heard footsteps behind her. She was too afraid to look around but she started walking faster, then running. She was not fast enough, and the guys caught up to her. One of them grabbed her by the arm and swung her around. He grabbed her purse and started pulling.

"Give me that!" he said. He was a guy who looked like he was not afraid to hurt someone. He tried to take the purse, but Hope's instincts took over and she pulled it away from him.

"Why, you . . . " he said, and he slapped her in the face. "Give it to me . . ." he said. Now he was mad. He made his fingers into a fist. The other guy just stood there, watching.

Brian was heading towards the park when he saw two guys and a girl ahead of him, but he could not tell from a distance who they were or what they were doing. As he got closer, he saw who the girl was: it was Hope, and one of the guys was about to hit her. He dropped the bag he was carrying, ran over to the guy standing over Hope, and he punched him right in the stomach.

"Brian!" screamed Hope, relieved and scared at the same time.

Brian stood in front of Hope while both guys advanced. The fight was two against one, but Brian punched and kicked and managed to hold his own. All of a sudden a police siren sang out, and the two guys took off.

Brian was still standing, but he looked like Frankenstein, all cut and bruised. He turned and faced Hope. "Are you OK?"

Hope just nodded.

"Good, then let's take you home," he said, turning around.

Hope saw that he was holding his side, and when he started walking, he fell down on the sidewalk. As she kneeled next to him, she saw that he was bleeding.

"Brian, we need to get you to a doctor," she said urgently.

"Don't worry—I've been through worse, but I think I do have to get home. Can you help me up?" he said, with a calm voice.

Hope didn't know what to say. She took his arm, put it around her neck, and helped him stand up.

"Thanks for helping me out," Brian said.

"It's the least I can do. You saved my life," she replied.

When they got to his house, Brian opened the door and pointed to the couch. "The couch is fine," he said.

After Hope helped him sit down, she told him, "I'll be right back," and she headed to the bathroom and opened the medicine cabinet. She took out a first-aid kit.

As she helped to clean and wrap Brian's wounds, he asked, "So why were they after you?"

"They wanted my purse," she replied.

"So why not give it to them?"

Hope said nothing. She opened her purse and took out a necklace on a thin gold chain. It had a small blue stone shaped like a heart.

Brian recognized the necklace—it had once belonged to his sister Grace. He remembered the day Grace gave Hope the necklace on her birthday. She gave it to Hope because Hope always admired it.

"How do you feel about what happened tonight?" he asked Hope.

She looked at him and said, "Nothing like this has ever happened to me. It makes me feel more determined to leave and find a new place to live."

"Why do you have so much hatred?" Brian asked.

"Look at what just happened to me today!" she shouted. "How can I feel good about this place when everything goes wrong in my life?"

He quietly said, "I know it hasn't been a great experience for you here, but I believe that if you try, you can find another side to this place. Think about the park: Has it all been that bad?"

Hope stayed silent for a few seconds, thinking about what he had just said. She knew that some things were good, like getting closer to Brian and helping the kids at the park.

"You have a point. I never thought that the inside of the park would look like it did," she admitted.

"You're getting close to them . . . " Brian started to say, as he had a great idea."Hey, Hope, can you do me a favor?"

"That depends," she answered.

"Well, with these cuts I won't be able to do much in the park. Would you mind helping me out there for a few more weeks?"

Hope was a bit scared; she didn't want to go back to that place, at least not right away. When she looked at Brian she remembered how he had defended her, even though it was just him against two others. If he had the courage to do that for her, the least she could do was face her fears and do what he was asking—besides, she did want to see the kids again.

"I'll do it," she said.

Brian saw that she was still afraid, so he said, "Don't worry, I'll call two of my friends; they'll go with you, as will I. You don't have to do it on your own."

"Thanks," she said, relieved that she was not going to have to go back by herself. As she thought about it, Hope started to have second thoughts about leaving. So much had happened: the death of her best friend, getting to know Brian, and most important, seeing a side of her neighborhood that she had never seen. She thought, "If the park had something hidden within, then can there be other great things hidden in other parts of this neighborhood that I've never seen? Maybe I should stay and see. I just hope Brian will be by my side."

Hope sat down next to him on the couch, and they spent most of the night talking about what she was going to do.

Two days later, Brian's friends James and Bob walked with Hope to the park; they were also were going to start helping there. Even with Brian's friends, Hope still felt a bit nervous about returning. Brian was at the park when they got there. After he gave James and Bob their assignments, they headed off, and Brian introduced the kids in the basketball gym to Hope. For the next few days Hope and Brian worked together. She was enjoying what she was doing, and she was getting closer and closer to Brian.

"So, do you still want to leave?" asked Brian, as they sat on a bench taking a breather.

"I don't know anymore," she said, looking at the sky. It was all cloudy as if it were going to rain.

"Well, I know that I would miss you if you left . . . besides, I think that there is a lot more for you to see."

"If you're the one helping me to see what I cannot, then maybe I will stay," she said.

They stared at each other for a few seconds, then Brian nodded his head. Hope smiled and stood up; she turned to Brian and put out her hand.

"Come on, there's a lot to do," she said. Brian smiled and replied, "Yes, there is a lot to do," and they walked together hand in hand.

JOURNAL ENTRIES
YVETTE MORENO

The Day We Met—August 1

It was a Saturday in August, and I was in school because I needed help in math. And that's where I met a new friend named Yameca. She came in after me, so she got the last chair—the one next to mine. She asked my name, and we started talking about our cultures. She was African-American, and I am Latina. She asked me what language I speak, and I told her I speak both Spanish and English. I asked her the languages she spoke, and she said only English. I told Yameca that I lived on Atlantic Street, and she said she lived on Hunter Street, a well-known street in Compton. I noticed her bracelet and asked her about it; she told me it was a special bracelet from Jamaica that her mother had given her. I could feel that we were going to connect as friends. We had things in common, like joking around in class and laughing loudly.

One Week Later—August 8

A new girl named Melanie came to class, and Yameca and I started making conversation with her. We asked each other questions so we could get to know each other. Yameca was very talkative, and Melanie was quiet until she saw we wanted to be friends with her, and then she started talking a lot. After that we hung out together, had lunch, and walked around the basketball courts. We didn't have any problems at first.

Two Weeks Later—August 22

We were outside in the parking lot waiting for our parents to pick us up. Melanie's mom arrived and asked Melanie if Yameca and I were her friends. She seemed angry, and she was staring at us. We wondered if she had a problem with us being her daughter's friends. Later Yameca called me and said she thought that Melanie's mom didn't like her because she was black; I thought Yameca was right, and it made me sad. I said that I didn't care, because we were still going to be friends no matter what.

The Next Day—August 23

Again we were in the parking lot waiting for our parents when suddenly Melanie told us to move away from her, but we didn't. Melanie's mom got out of the car and screamed things at Yameca and me. She said, "Stupid little girls! You will never be friends with Melanie! Dumb girls!" We stood quiet and surprised, because we never thought this could happen—not in this lifetime. I had never experienced a mom disapproving of her daughter's friends because of their color and culture. Later, Yameca called me and got a third line on the phone for Melanie, but Melanie's mom found out, took away the phone, and hung up.

The Day After That—August 24

Yameca asked Melanie what had happened. Yameca embarrassed Melanie, but she didn't answer. We changed the subject. As the day passed, we didn't talk about the problem anymore.

Two Weeks Later—September 7

We still didn't say anything about the problem between us, but then Melanie told us she needed to give us some bad news. She said that her mom told her that she was tired of telling Melanie to stop talking to us. She said they were going to move to a different neighborhood and that Melanie's mom was going to send her to a different school.

Three Weeks Later—September 28

Melanie told us it was the last time we would see her; she also said her mom was changing their home phone number. She was very sad because her mom was forcing her to move.

Today—November 25

It's been almost two months since the last time I saw Melanie; I miss my friend. I wish I could call her, but I don't have her new number. I hope I get to see her again someday.

I hope that other parents in Los Angeles realize how wonderful it is to have their children meet friends from other cultures and backgrounds.

DREAM DANCE
JACKELYN GOMEZ

Desiree is looking around outside the Roosevelt High School gym. It is
8 PM on a Saturday night. There is a line of students, all dressed up for
the Sadie Hawkins dance, heading inside—this is a dance where you
and your girlfriends, all dressed the same way, go together. Desiree can
hear her favorite songs coming from inside the gym. She pays for her
ticket and enters the room, and she sees ten other girls dressed just like
her: cowgirls, all in black, with knee-high cowboy boots and J-Lo, stylish
cowboy hats, with their hair down.

They are the popular girls, and Desiree is one of them

Tiffany, the most popular of the popular girls, grabs Desiree's hand
and pulls her into the center of the crowd to dance in a circle with the
rest of the "cowgirls." They are dancing, and Desiree realizes she has
never felt the way she is feeling—she is feeling that she is alive!

This is Desiree's first time dancing. At first she is embarrassed, but
the more she dances, the more she gets the rhythm of the music. Then a
guy comes over and asks her if she would like to dance with him. All of
the girls are telling her to say yes, so she does. The other popular girls are
all looking at her. She feels important, like these girls are her true friends.

The song stops, and they stop dancing; she thanks the guy for dancing with her. The Sadie Hawkins dance is now over, and its time to take
pictures. All ten girls come together, and they ask her if she wants to be
photographed with them as a group for the yearbook. They pose for the
picture, making funny faces for the camera, and suddenly the flash of the
camera wakes Desiree up.

She looks around and realizes she is not in the gym, but in her AP
Calculus class, and she feels sad. The ten popular girls are in the class, all
sitting around Desiree. They are all talking about going to the dance and
what they will be wearing. The Sadie Hawkins dance is not until tomorrow night, but Desiree knows she is not going.

Instead, Desiree will be going to a birthday party for her Mom's
best friend's son, next door to her house. Desiree's five sisters and little

brother will be going along too. She doesn't really want to go to the birthday party, but she doesn't want to go to the dance alone, either.

The bell rings for fourth period, and it's time to go home. As Desiree is packing her stuff to leave, Tiffany comes by her desk and asks her if she is going to go the dance, and Desiree says no. Then to her surprise, Tiffany asks her if she would like to go with them—and she says yes! Tiffany describes how they are going to dress as cowgirls. Desiree realizes that her first L.A. dream has come true: she has found new friends.

THE SILVER LINING
CHRISTIAN OLIVA

Los Angeles, known for its courageous leaders and talented artists, is a place that can destroy your spirit if you allow it, or it can make your dreams come true—if you're up to the challenge.

This is the story of a Los Angeles family made up of a father and three siblings: Lily, Darren, and Terry. Sadly, Lily's mother had passed away after giving birth to her, and Lily never got to feel her love and warm praise. Nonetheless, Lily, who was eight years old, was enjoying life without a care in the world; she was being raised and loved properly by her two brothers. The children's father was always busy, trying to provide for his children by himself, something that is extremely difficult to accomplish in L.A. Since his wife's death he had become an abusive alcoholic who put his friends and his own personal needs before his family, and he always had to be high in order to accomplish his daily tasks. He didn't know how to care for his family, and in the end he was pitied and despised by them. Luckily, Terry, the first-born son, was maturing into a responsible young man who took charge of caring for his brother and sister whenever their father was gone. Terry had always been a gifted child who had been influenced positively by his teachers and his mentors.

✳

It turned out to be an unforgettable evening on the notorious streets of Los Angeles, although it had been a beautiful day like any other. It was an extra-special treat to have Terry at home preparing supper for the family. Terry was an engineering student at a local college, and he had his own apartment, but he loved to cook for his family and search out new recipes. Darren had gone to the local grocery store to purchase vegetables and spices for their meal, while Lily played outside, enjoying the breeze as it blew through her hair. She was picking flowers, waiting for the sunset. Suddenly the breeze was gone, and Lily heard the familiar honking that always brought a smile to her face. The honking indicated that the *raspadero* was near. The *raspaderos* scraped ice off a huge ice block and served it in a Styrofoam cup, adding flavors to make a delicious cool treat. She immediately began to sprint towards the *raspadero*, who had paused beneath some shade.

As Darren returned from the market, holding the finishing touches to the dinner waiting at home, he glanced at the sunset; its glow made his neighborhood even more beautiful. He ignored the cars as they raced down the street. As always at that time of day, like any other normal day, local neighbors, gangsters, acquaintances, and friends stood in their usual places. Darren passed a couple of freeloaders named Lencho and Chuy who liked to take what didn't belong to them, but they never asked Darren for anything. Then he walked by a couple of gangsters who were always on the move because they feared that if they stopped, trouble would catch up to them. Other neighbors sat on their front porches, engaged in *chismiando,* gossiping. As he reached a familiar tree, he noticed that Lily was a block away, buying a *raspado.* As he approached her, he could hear the loud engine of a car advancing along the curved street, not yet in sight; this seemed weird to Darren, because no one raced along the curved, narrow street that fast until late at night.

Suddenly a blue car appeared, chased by a roaring SUV. Puzzled and worried for his sister, he caught a glance of the SUV, moving at a high speed from behind the car, heading towards the curve. Assuming that the two cars were going to collide, Darren dropped the bag of groceries as he ran, shouting to the drivers to slow down and be careful—but it was too late to avoid the vicious catastrophe.

The SUV flipped over when it dipped into a pothole, and the driver turned sharply, trying to avoid a collision. The blue vehicle slammed into the SUV as it flipped, striking numerous cars and a nearby light post in its path, causing glass and sparks to fly as it came to rest next to the tree where Lily was standing. Lily was thrown into the car's windshield, which, as it shattered, cut her severely.

A split second after the incident, the whole neighborhood seemed to be out on the street, as if a parade were passing through. Some were on the phone calling 911, while others simply observed the horrific scene with shock and disgust. (The cause of the accident was common carelessness, ignorance, and drug abuse, all of which are seen daily on these streets—people need to use self-control and take responsibility for their actions.)

The paramedics arrived quickly and took Lily, who was barely breathing, to the hospital.

At the hospital, Terry and Darren waited anxiously for the doctor's report on Lily's condition. As Terry went to get coffee, Darren sat alone with his feelings of guilt; he felt especially responsible because he was the main person in charge of Lily's care since Terry had left for college and their father was usually gone. Terry returned with two cups of coffee.

"Lily doesn't have health insurance," whispered Terry.

"I know, but I'm sure we'll find some way to sort this out," replied Darren. "The important thing is that she is still alive," he added.

Then the door to the emergency room swung open, and Dr. Alvarez stepped outside.

"We've done all we can. Lily received a major blow to the head and is in a coma; we don't know exactly when she'll wake up. We hope her brain injury isn't too serious," he said. "She's stable and will need some time to recover, but she's lucky that none of her other vital organs were damaged."

The two brothers remained at the hospital for hours, trying to think of a way to pay for Lily's medical care. "I've got it!" said Terry.

"What? What is it?" asked Darren as he jumped to his feet.

"It's perfect—it might take a while to do it, but it will be well worth it," said Terry. "We can create a car that runs on electricity, corn oil, and solar power."

"What the hell are you talking about? Create a car? Out of what?" asked Darren.

Terry then told his brother about his engineer and chemist friends from college who had already built a different kind of hybrid car and who would help them build theirs. He convinced them to get involved by showing them an example of the power of corn oil to run a customized engine that he had built from scratch. Terry's college friends felt terrible about Lily's accident, so most volunteered to work for free on this intriguing project. However, creating the car itself would cost money, like everything else in Los Angeles, so the boys decided to mortgage the house in order to begin building the car.

After six months of hard work, the car was almost completed—however, there was a crucial piece of the project missing: a gyrator that would whirl the reusable fuel in place so that the car would actually move. They still didn't have enough money to pay Lily's hospital bill, which continued to grow larger, but the project was going great so they remained hopeful. If they were able to come up with the gyrator for their car, they felt sure it would sell, and they would make millions.

One afternoon the boys decided call it a day since it was too hot to do much work and hardly any of their colleagues had shown up. They decided that they'd go out for an ice and go cruise the streets, but as they were beginning to clean up the garage and put their tools away, the phone rang: it was a nurse from the hospital calling to inform them that Lily was awake.

The boys were thrilled that Lily had finally emerged from her coma. When they arrived, Lily was so happy to see them—she just wanted to give them big hugs, so they hugged her tight and kissed her softly. Lily was far from fully recovered and she needed further surgery, but at that moment she was a little girl who was simply happy to see her big brothers; Terry and Darren, in turn, were overjoyed to hear Lily's soft voice again. They knew that now, more than ever, they had to finish their prototype and begin working to help Lily get well.

While the siblings were celebrating, Lily's doctor was watching the love spread through the room. He was impressed by how much these two young men cared for their little sister. He felt like this family was something special.

As visiting hours ended, Lily fell asleep after listening to the boys talk about all that had happened over the past six months; they promised Lily they'd be back tomorrow, and they headed home. As they got close to their neighborhood, they heard the sound of sirens, and as they rounded a curve, they saw a huge crowd in the street. People were straining to get a better view of something they could not see—although they could see smoke—so they paused and tried to get the attention of a man who was walking away.

"Excuse me!" called Darren from the open car window. "What's going on up there?"

"There's a house burning down! It's a huge fire!" yelled the guy.

Darren and Terry looked at each other—the fire was in the direction of their house. They quickly jumped out of the car, leaving it in the middle of the street, and started to run toward the commotion. As they pushed through the crowd, they came across Lencho. He grabbed Darren's shoulder.

"Hey man, your *cantón* is on fire!" shouted Lencho. Even thugs like Lencho cared about the well-being of this family, which certainly didn't need another tragedy.

"*Serio*! But how?" asked Darren, still making his way through the people clustered in the street. Darren and Terry made it to the edge of the crowd—even though they were stopped in their tracks by the yellow tape that read, "Caution," they could see that their house was in flames, and the garage was up in smoke.

"Oh, no! The car!" yelled Terry.

Without thinking, the boys ducked under the tape and started to run towards the garage, but they were stopped by a police officer who held them back. "Hey," said the policeman, "what are you doing? You can't go in there."

"But we live here!" cried Darren.

"I'm sorry, boys, but it's dangerous. You have to step back. The firefighters are doing everything they can."

The cop walked them back behind the yellow tape. Darren and Terry were in shock. They couldn't believe that this disaster had occurred when they were so close to finishing their project. They stood there and watched as their house burned down to the ground. How could the fire have started?

After the flames were finally out, the fire captain came to talk to them.

"I'm so sorry," the captain said. "We tried to save the structures, but there was nothing we could do; this fire was really strong. The neighbors heard a loud bang coming from the garage. We know the fire started there and then spread to the house."

"Do you know if it was electrical?" asked Terry.

"No, it wasn't," replied the captain. "It seemed like it was being fed by something in the garage."

Darren and Terry knew that something to do with the car had started the fire. They thought back: Recently, one of the chemistry students helping with the car had brought along some strong chemicals for a different project he was working on, and he'd forgotten them in the garage. It had been really hot that day—maybe the chemicals had reacted with the heat and caused an explosion? It didn't really matter. The house and the garage and the car were all gone.

What were they going to do? That night, at Terry's apartment, the boys slept on it. In the morning, as they realized that they had no money, no equipment, and no garage, they knew it was going to be a long day.

They began the day by paying Lily the visit they had promised her; Darren knew it would cheer her and them up. When they arrived at the hospital, Lily was in physical therapy, so they had to wait. The boys sat down, talked about their situation, and started brainstorming, each focusing on different tasks. As they discussed different strategies that would allow them to buy what they needed and start over again on another engine, Dr. Alvarez overheard their unique plans—and he thought that their ideas were great.

Dr. Alvarez, who had always been dedicated to his career and never had children of his own, was a very good investor and had managed to amass a small fortune. He admired Terry and Darren for their hard work and optimism, as well as their closeness with their sister, and right then and there he decided that he would offer to invest in Terry's idea. He was impressed with how well thought-out the boys' plans were—and besides, he was happy to help the family out, if only for Lily's sake

Dr. Alvarez approached Terry and Darren. "Good morning," he said, "it's nice to see both of you again."

"Good morning," responded the boys.

"Lily will be back from therapy soon," said the doctor. "In the meanwhile, why don't you tell me the rest of your plans for this car. I've been listening to your ideas, and I'm interested in helping you out as an investor in the project—I think it could be really successful."

At first Terry and Darren were surprised and overwhelmed by the doctor's generous offer. Dr. Alvarez assured them that he not only wanted to help the family, but he also believed in their work—and he never missed the opportunity to make a good investment. It was actually a perfect fit: Dr. Alvarez already had an amazing car collection, and he even offered one of his favorite cars to use as the body of the new prototype. The three of them would become business partners and grow the company together.

The boys began to believe that maybe everything would be OK. Psyched about the rebirth of the project—and realizing that they had been blessed—they spent a wonderful morning with Lily and Dr. Alvarez.

After three months of intensive work, the new car was finished —and Darren and Terry were thrilled with the final outcome (Dr. Alvarez was also very pleased). They took the vehicle, which they named "The Silver Lining," to a car show at Staples Center, and it was the star of the show. All the major car manufacturers wanted in on this hip, environmentally beneficial car. The brothers and the doctor eventually established partnerships with Pontiac and Mitsubishi, and they opened up dealerships all over California and the world. Soon everybody was driving a Silver Lining, which changed the entire city of Los Angeles with its environmental benefits. The smog that surrounded the city disappeared, the sky was clear, and everyone could breathe more easily.

The company ultimately became so successful that it generated more than enough money to pay all of Lily's hospital bills, buy a new house, and set up college funds for all three of the siblings—and then some. With the extra money, the brothers set up a fund that would allow other kids in the neighborhood to go to college as well, because they felt that education and knowledge were some of life's greatest gifts.

As much as it improved the environment and their financial situation, the car did something even better for Darren, Terry, and Lily. Their father was so amazed and impressed by his sons' success that he entirely changed his ways. He got rid of all his bad habits and went to work for his sons, becoming a great asset to the company and to their family.

This family's story symbolizes life in Los Angeles and the hardships found in the real world, but perhaps from this inspiring example of how to cope with tragedy we can learn that anything is possible if we work hard to create change. Darren, Terry, and all their collaborators made an effort to better the community they lived in, and their positive influence was felt by many.

Without one another, we have nothing. Together we have everything.

'TIL YOU COME HOME, WE'LL BE WAITING
STEPHANIE VELASQUEZ

Dear brother,

Do you know how much I miss you? I know I haven't written to you for a long time, but that does not mean that I don't think about you. On Monday I was watching a TV show about prison, and I thought of you. The young man in jail, Michael, reminded me of you, so I watched the whole two-hour show. Now every Monday I watch that show.

Yesterday I went to the Football Classic. This year it was held at East L.A. College. It was really fun, even though Roosevelt lost. I really wish you could have been there—I know you used to like going every year. I have been thinking that you will not be with us for Thanksgiving, and that makes me very sad. I was sure that this year you would be home. I remember how quiet it was without you last year—you were the one who was always making jokes and teasing every one in the family.

When you get out, everything will go back to normal. We will have dinner together and make jokes. I'll leave for school in the morning, and just as I'm about to walk out the door, you will tell me, "Hey, take care" —and those words will mean so much to me. I know you'll be there for me. I will no longer feel like a part of me is missing. But every time you come back home, you disappoint me by going back to your old self, the one that doesn't think about the people who care about you and who will suffer for your mistakes.

Every time the phone rings and the caller ID says "PRISON," it's like a fire alarm ringing. We all want to answer it before it hangs up. We all want to know if something happened, we want to know any news about you. Mom worries so much.

Hey foo', you need to start behaving in there. When you suffer, we suffer even more. Do you know why? Because we can't do anything to help you. I remember once when mom was crying; I was kind of used to it, but this time she had been crying all night. She told me that something awful had happened, but she didn't tell me because I preferred not to know. I remember how you told us you thought you were going crazy, and the only thing that saved you was the Bible. I really wish you would think about what you do before you do it. I wish you could think about us, your family, the people you hurt, and the people who are waiting here patiently and anxiously for you to come home.

Love,

Alelie

HURT
ERIK ESTEVEZ

Downtown Los Angeles is one of my favorite places in the world—not that I've seen much of the world. Sunrise was still hours away, and the streets were flooded with a morning mist instead of people. The sky was dark, and only a few stars shone thanks to the city lights. The aroma of the mist mixed with the stench of the homeless, creating a foul but somewhat welcoming smell.

I made my way down the apartment stairway, my pack stuffed with posters and my photos. I thought about what I was about to do, whether or not it really worth the risk, but these thoughts were blown away the moment I stepped out and the freezing wind hit my face. All that mattered was where I would begin. A few moments later I was making my way up Spring Street toward Fourth, to the area of the city that had acquired names like Bumville, Tent Town, and Cardboard Plaza.

After a few blocks I spotted where the first flyer would go—it was a pay phone missing the receiver. The flyer pictured a number of people who had set up camp in front of a closed-down homeless shelter. The only witnesses to my petty crime were those who are regarded as "the scum of society" by those who would rather drop a couple of coins in their hands than make eye contact. These "scum" paid little or no attention to me, with the exception of a couple of lowlifes who seemed to be under the influence.

"Oooh, I'm telling," the younger-looking of the two shouted. This was followed by an irritating laugh that made the hairs on the back of my neck rise. "Police . . . police. There is a man here vandalizing the city," shouted the other. His voice had a raspy sound to it, which led me to believe he was a chain-smoker.

At first their calls made me uneasy, but as time went on it became clear that no one was taking them seriously. I wiped the sweat of paranoia from my forehead and continued posting the flyers on the sides of buildings as I made my way up Fourth Street. Seeing those two lowlifes together brought back memories of Victor and me: How we would take "self-motivated field trips" during first period to the fast-food joint, just for some breakfast; how we spent countless afternoons smoking while discussing the latest drama in our lives. Then I thought of how I had stood over his open grave, with my fist full of dirt. Funny how screwing up your life doesn't seem like a big deal as long as you do it with someone else.

❋

The last time Victor and I spoke to one another as two somewhat clear-minded individuals, we were on his porch. I remember because it was right before my folks put me on the bus to military school. It was something they had threatened to do since the first time the principal suspended me for smoking in the restroom.

"What?! You mean they're actually sending you away?" Vic asked. He was leaning against the wall.

"Yeah, they just told me a few minutes ago," I replied. I sat on the top step with my head in my hands.

"But, but how?" He didn't know whether to laugh or cry—that, or he honestly didn't believe I'd be going away for a long time.

"Listen, it came as a surprise to me, too. I mean, I walked into the living room to find my folks and David waiting for me."

David's my older brother. At the age of twelve he was running around the neighborhood causing trouble; by sixteen he was in a gang and smoking crack; two years later he was one of the main gang leaders. Then, at the age of twenty-six, he became a victim of a drive-by shooting that claimed the lives of two of his homies. He was lucky—he only had to spend a few days in the hospital.

I kicked an empty can of RC Cola to the street. "I could tell by the way my father was standing that he had found my stash," I said.

"Jesus, man, how many times did I tell you never to leave your #$%* stash lying around? Or at least find a better hiding place than underneath your mattress," he remarked while slumping to the floor.

"I know David was the one who put the idea of military school into their heads. Damn hypocrite, he reads the Bible once and he thinks he's a saint," I said.

After the shooting David claimed he had changed into a church man—the same guy who used to chug a beer while peeing on the steps of the church every New Year's. "Well, once I saw the duffel bag and the bus ticket, I knew they weren't joking." I stood up and cracked my neck.

"They didn't want to let me come say good-bye, but they knew they couldn't stop me."

"Damn, so you're really leaving." Victor's tone had changed, as if reality had finally sunk in.

"Yeah . . . but hey, the joke's on them, 'cause I'll be out in ten months," I replied, trying to sound reassuring.

"What do you mean?" he asked, standing up.

"In ten months I'll be eighteen and a legal adult," I answered with a smile. "I'll just simply pull myself out of that school."

This seemed to give him hope. "Yeah, but that's still ten months away. You think you can survive?"

"I hope so, or else I am doomed," I said sarcastically. "You want to know what the worst part of this is? They're not even letting me say good-bye to Grace." Grace was my kid sister. She and I were close; she came to me for guidance, and I went to her for comfort.

At that very moment, my father's sedan pulled up in front of Vic's house. I hugged him good-bye and started towards the car that would take me to the bus station and the place where I would spend ten months of my life.

✱

I turned onto Sixth Street. It was still freezing cold. The darkness and thick mist helped cover my actions from the few who had taken to the streets for a light jog. My pack was starting to feel lighter. After a few blocks I reached Fourth Street and the location of the billboard. It displayed an ad that promised you the time of your life with beautiful women after a night of drinking.

✱

Once ten months had passed, I did just as I said I would: I checked myself out and walked away from military school. I bought a bus ticket with the money I'd scraped together over time. When I arrived in the City of Angels, I realized how much can change in a short period of time. I headed straight to my old elementary school in hopes of finding the one person I had longed to see for what felt like an eternity.

As I waited, I wondered whether or not she had grown since the last time I had seen her. Perhaps I wouldn't even recognize her, or maybe she wouldn't recognize me. I was growing impatient as I waited in front of the main entrance for the bell to ring. I thought back to the days when I had spent the entire day waiting to be dismissed. It really is depressing when you think about it: I mean, I wasted the entire day just waiting for it to end.

After some time the bell did ring and the youngsters poured out of the doorway like a stampede of wild beasts. This made spotting Grace impossible. In all the commotion, I did not notice that she had found me and had somehow made her way to my side.

"I'm waiting," she said.

"Huh, where did you come from?" I asked.

"Uh, I don't know. School maybe?" she answered.

I knelt down and pulled her into my arms, and we held each other tight for who knows how long. She held my hand as we walked home. Along the way she told me of all the things she'd been up to while I was gone. When we reached home, she stopped.

"Do they know you're back?" She looked scared, as if my return was a crime.

"No," I answered "Why? What do you think they'll say?"

She paused for a moment, then breathed in and continued toward the house. Nine years of age and already she understood what my return meant.

✳

The morning mist was beginning to fade away, which meant I had to speed up if I was going to climb onto the billboard undetected. I had seen this beer ad a few days ago and knew this was the best location for my poster. Climbing the fence was simple; it was the jump from the top of the fence to the billboard ladder that was difficult. Nevertheless, I reached the top and hung the posters, which showed the increase in underage drinking in areas of poverty.

Staring at the model's smile as she danced to an unheard beat while holding a beer bottle reminded me of better days. Vic and I would walk around the neighborhood Saturday nights searching for a house party we could crash. Most nights we came up empty, and we would find ourselves in his room watching whatever caught our attention on TV. When we did stumble upon a party, it was usually a family gathering to celebrate a birthday or something. Vic and I would wait for the party to reach its peak to make our move. We would walk in with the intention of drinking a few beers when no one was looking and meeting some girls; at the very least, we hoped to gain a few phone numbers. These memories of recklessness kept me sane in those godforsaken ten months away.

�֍

Everything went as I thought it would: my folks became hysterical the moment I walked through the front door, and David began ranting about how ungrateful I was for not staying in the school they had spent so much money on. Luckily Grace didn't see any of this; she'd dodged into her room the minute we stepped into the house. The shouting ceased in a matter of time; I guess they figured out that no matter how loud they got, it wouldn't change the fact that I was home.

"I just can't believe you would do this. Didn't you once think that it was for your own good?" asked David.

"No," I answered with a proud smile. "Do you know when Vic will be home?"

At the sound of his name David froze, which made me uneasy. "About Vic—listen, he's gone through a few changes since you left . . . " his tone was that of a mortician, cold and serious.

"What do you mean?" I asked.

David explained to me that during our time apart, Vic had taken a turn for the worse. His "habits" had increased to the point of being constant. He told me that he couldn't even picture Vic without a joint. I ran out of the house in disbelief.

When I reached Vic's street, I learned that his situation was even worse than David had led me to believe. It seems Vic had outgrown marijuana and had begun looking elsewhere for relief: "Cocaine and heroin had taken over his soul," is how his younger cousin put it.

"Oh, how good it is to see you, Alonso. Please come in." Vic's mom was always polite to everyone, but in the end it was her gentle spirit that allowed Vic to slowly kill himself. She just couldn't bring herself to see the truth. "When did you arrive?"

"I just got back," I answered. The house was a mess, which was odd, since Vic's mom could win housekeeping tournaments with her tidiness. "Where's Vic?" I asked.

"I'm right here." Vic appeared in the kitchen doorway. He looked like he hadn't rested since I left. "What's going on?"

"Just wanted to see you—long time, you know?" I answered. Even though I had been expecting it, I was still taken aback by his appearance.

His body resembled that of a starving Third World refugee, and the bags under his eyes dragged dark.

"Oh . . ." he said. An awkward silence followed. "Come on, let's go to my room."

His room was just as it was the day I left, a complete mess. He threw himself on the bed, which was littered with aging newspapers. "So what's new?" he asked, focusing on the stained ceiling.

I plopped myself down on a pile of dirty laundry. "That's a question I should be asking you."

"What do you mean?" He was trying his hardest to sound sincere.

"Vic! I've known you since fifth grade—you couldn't lie to me then either." I was growing tired of his reluctance to answer the question. "So why not save us both some time and just tell me what's wrong now."

He scrambled to his feet in a fit of rage, shouting "Goddamn it, Alonso, nothing is wrong with me, OK?! Listen, I'm not some charity case for you or anyone else to worry about." He fell back onto his bed and said, "The last thing I need right now is someone bringing me down, so if you're going to keep on preaching, then leave."

I walked out, shutting the door behind me. I was making my way towards the front door when I noticed that his mom hadn't moved. She looked disappointed. I figured she was counting on my return to be the miracle that brought her son back from limbo.

She walked me to the door. "Please excuse him. He's just a bit under the weather. Perhaps you could return tomorrow when he's feeling better."

"Oh, OK." I left their house without saying anything else.

✻

The view from this height was amazing. The mist was mostly gone, and what did remain would be gone in a matter of moments. The streetlights were all turned off, and the sidewalks were stirring with people, mostly vendors who were setting up their shops for the swarms of people who would be looking for the best bargain. The sky that once cast a protective shadow was now bright. I climbed down, not wanting to attract attention, for now more than ever time was of the essence.

✻

The following morning I received a message from Vic apologizing for his behavior the day before and asking me to meet him at his house. When I arrived, he was sitting on his front steps drinking a cup of coffee and smoking a cigarette, his routine breakfast.

"Hey, you feeling any better?" I asked. "Because you still look like #$%*." I kept my distance, for some reason.

"Holy #$%*, it's good to see you," he replied. "Well, aren't you going to give me a hug?"

We held each other tight for who knows how long. "OK, that's enough of that," he said with a smile.

"I figure you don't remember much of yesterday?" I asked as I took a seat on the steps.

"To be honest, no, no I don't. All my mom said was, you came to see me and I dozed off . . . " He turned to face me. "But I'm damn sure there's more to it than that, am I right?" He took a sip from the mug, which read, "Happy Mother's Day." "So just let me say I'm sorry if I challenged you to a fight, if I puked or slobbered on you, if I cursed you out or whatever. Point is, I'm sorry, OK?"

"Wait, how can you be sorry for something you don't even remember doing?"

"Alonso, it is too early in the morning for you to be asking questions like that. You want some? Black with sugar, your favorite," he said, pushing the mug towards me.

"Sure." I took the mug from him and took a sip. "It's good."

Vic began coughing but soon got it under control. "Yeah, it is good." He let a small cough out before spitting out mucus.

"You alright?" I asked, knowing he wasn't.

"Yeah, you know me, I'm always good." He was trying to pull it off, but then realized he couldn't even fool himself. "No, I'm not alright. I'm not even close."

"No #$%*, the dead are healthier than you, and they look better too," I said. "So you want to fill me in on what you've been doing these past few months?"

"What for? You probably already heard it from everyone else," he said, turning to face me. I could tell he was pissed off about people talking about him and his "habits" as if it were a TV drama.

"What? You're angry at me for wanting to understand what happened to my friend?" I asked.

"Well, you know me, Alonso. It's dangerous to leave me alone with my thoughts." I knew exactly what he meant: you see, Vic wasn't in mint condition even before I left. I guess his absent father and abusive stepfather might have had something to do with it. "When you left it was like reality came and smacked me around like I owed it money."

"Hey, it was hard for me too." It really was—not only was I separated from those I cared for, but I also wasn't allowed any visitors my folks hadn't authorized. "The whole time I was there, all I thought about was when I'd be able to leave that place."

"Yeah, I know it was hard for you, but you had something to look forward to. I mean, when you left, everything I enjoyed lost all meaning. I began thinking about where I was headed in life."

"So you got depressed and thought shooting up was going to change it?" I said. "Is that what you're telling me?"

"Yes. I mean no . . ." he said, and lowered his head. "See, you don't understand." The moment that followed seemed to drag on for hours. Then he simply stood up. "Let's take a walk."

We walked in silence for the first few blocks; neither of us had much to say to one another at the time. Soon we found ourselves near South Park, a breeding ground for dealers and users alike. We walked over to the old willow tree that stood next to a picnic table. In the past we had come to smoke away the day in its shade.

Vic leaned against the tree and stared out at the lonely playing field. "I didn't give up," he said. "I tried getting a job and going to school."

I sat on the picnic table looking at him. "So what happened?"

A smirk formed on his face. "Do you remember when we would spend hours here just talking about the day we would leave this place?" He turned to face me. "We were just going to jump on our Harleys and ride into the sunrise away from everyone and everything."

Vic was talking about the dream we had thought up after an afternoon of smoking. It was that dream that got us through high school. Whenever he and I fell into a slump, we would just think of how sometime soon we would be on that highway, and it would provide just enough hope to keep us from slitting our wrists.

"Yeah . . . I remember," I replied. "You know we're still going to, right?"

"I know. Anyway, like I was saying, the first couple of months were hard but I was dealing with it. I was looking for a job, figured I should have some cash in case you broke out and we needed to leave fast. And I was taking some college courses over at Trade Tech," he said, while gazing into the sky.

This was the first positive thing that I had heard from him since my return. "So what stopped you?" I asked.

"Life and all the #$%* it brings." He took a deep breath and let it out slowly. "I couldn't get a job because I didn't have any experience; either that or it was because of my record. Soon the bills began to mount, and I knew my mom couldn't cover it all. So I dropped the courses and got a job working in a factory, sewing, making nothing an hour."

"Wait, what about Dan? Wasn't he helping with the bills?" Dan was the stepfather.

"That deadbeat ran out on us about a month after you left," he answered.

"I see. You couldn't pay the bills and you thought taking up heroin would help," I said, looking at him.

"When you say it like that, it sounds stupid," he replied with a smirk. "No, I'm afraid it's more complicated than that. You see, even with that job we still couldn't make the rent on time. And if you thought getting a job at the sweatshop was tough, it was impossible for me to find another one."

"So what did you do?" I asked. But I knew what he had done. He had gone to see Steve, a dealer we had come to know.

"You know what I did." He turned and stared at me with a look of disappointment. "I know you spoke to Steve. Damn it, don't talk to me as if you're a psychiatrist and I'm some head case." He spat at the ground, then shouted, "man, I've known you how long? And you chose to talk to me like that?" He turned away from me and drove his fist into the willow.

I stood up and kept him from further damaging his knuckles. "Hey, he didn't say much. Besides, you know I don't trust him," I responded.

"Why? 'Cause he's a drug dealer?" he shouted.

He was so quick to respond, I figured I had struck a chord; this was good because it meant there was still some sort of fight left in him. "Yeah, because he's a drug dealer who got bro into #$%* he couldn't handle."

"Hey, I can handle myself just fine," he blurted out.

Then he realized how stupid he sounded and lowered his head into his hands.

"So this is what you call handling it?" I knelt down so that our eyes met. "Listen, all he said was that you went to him for some work and ended up being his most reliable customer."

We spent the rest of the day clearing the air and reminiscing about our high-school years. We visited all of the old hangouts in search of a couple of girls to keep us entertained, but with no success. Neither of us had a driver's license—or a car, for that matter—so we simply hung out at his house, making plans for the future. Around midafternoon he headed off to work, and I headed to the entrance of Main Street Elementary. As I lingered on the steps waiting for the bell, I was "urged" to wait across the street from the school by a police officer—turns out some teachers had complained about a suspicious-looking individual. Once Grace was released, we spent the rest of the day celebrating her belated birthday.

The next day I went looking for Vic; the night before we had made plans to meet up early to discuss our future. The images of that morning are forever carved into my mind. Even before I entered the room, I already knew. Honestly, how could I not? All the signs were there. The only question was, when?

To Alonso,

I hope to god that it is you who finds me before anyone else does. I hate that I'm wishing this burden on you. The thing is, you, my friend, my brother, are the only one I have ever been able to count on. Funny how my last request comes to you from the other side. Well, I doubt it will seem funny at first, but over time, who knows. God, I hope they don't come to you and ask something stupid like why I did it or something like that. And keep them from trying to portray me as some sort of lost sheep or an angel that just lost his way. I always hated it when the TV news would show stories about gang members or those stupid criminals who ended up being killed by the cops or gang members killed by another gang idiot. The way I see it, you live by the gun, you die by the gun. I knew the consequences of my actions, so don't you let them say otherwise. Damn, these are my final words to you and I'm ranting on as if I was to see you tomorrow. The point of these suicide letters is to set the record straight, so I just want to say that. For some reason I can't seem to put together the words to say what I feel. It's like I hurt, I hurt all the time when I'm awake. When I'm sleeping it doesn't make a difference. It's like I'm strapped to a chair facing a blank screen, and every once in a while the screen runs a clip of a time I either disappointed someone, made an ass out of myself, hurt someone I loved, or all of them at once. This would happen to me throughout the day, making it a living hell. I can't go on with my life, knowing it will continue to be this way, I just can't. I know it sounds like I'm giving up, but I don't care— I just can't go on. Please forgive me for anything I did to you, and believe me when I say I never intended to hurt you. You know how we were talking about how Bob Marley's "Stop that Train" was our soundtrack? Well, I've been thinking it over, and I've come to the conclusion that I relate more to Johnny Cash's remake of "Hurt." Those lyrics just say what I've been struggling to say in this poor excuse of a letter. Now I know why most people choose not to leave one. No matter how long or how much we try, something is bound to be left unsaid.

Sincerely, your brother

Victor Rendon

p.s. Tell my mom I'm sorry for everything and that my last thoughts were of her.

He was clutching this letter when I found him—even in death he couldn't bear to admit how he felt. The syringe on the floor told me everything I needed to know. I knew he wouldn't want his mom to see him like that, so I straightened his motionless body across his bed, which for once was made; then I wiped the blood off his hand; and finally, I shut his eyes. Word spread fast of his death once the ambulance arrived and they carried him out. David came as soon as he heard.

"Hey, uh, listen, I know I didn't think the world of him, but know I'm sorry he's dead," he said, placing his hand on my shoulder. This is exactly what Vic wanted me to avoid.

I was the one who broke the news to Ms. Rendon. She took it surprisingly well. She didn't break down into tears or anything. Nor did I, for that matter. We weren't suppressing our pain; we just understood the truth of our reality. Vic's wake and funeral were held a short time after that—it was more like a gathering of those who had failed him when he had needed them the most: relatives he hadn't seen since he was a toddler showed up with tears dripping down their checks; neighbors came who were probably talking ill of him while he lay there bleeding to death. Long story short, in single file they paid their last respects, the casket was lowered, people wept, and after a while, one by one, they began to climb back into their cars and drive away. Soon only Ms. Rendon and I remained. A few days later a tombstone was laid down. It read: "Here lies Victor Rendon, 1984–2001, beloved son and friend."

※

It's amazing how a city can completely change in such a short period of time. Only a few hours ago these streets were at peace, free of any disturbance. Now, just minutes after sunrise, those same streets were packed with people going to work or wherever they needed to be. In the months that followed Vic's death, I found myself in a hole I couldn't climb out of. Three events changed that, though. The first was being thrown out by my father, which left me no choice but to take refuge at Ms. Rendon's house.

The second was Grace being sent away to live with my aunt and uncle in Phoenix in hopes it would keep her from turning out like David and me. The third was realizing that I had lost everyone and everything I held dear—therefore, I had nothing left to lose.

At the moment, I'm enjoying my routine breakfast of a cup of coffee followed by a cigarette. Before you start lecturing me on the consequences, know that I am already fully aware of them. I guess that's the reason lung cancer patients and victims don't get a ribbon.

I was staring at the public's reaction to my photos. Some stopped to look, purely out of curiosity, while others just simply walked past them. I was heading back to my apartment when a young man caught my attention. He was about sixteen years old, and from the looks of it he was heading to school. He stood staring at my photograph of an overfilled trash can in front of an elementary school. Then, in one swift move, he tore it down and walked away.

DEAR MAYOR
JULISSA ACOSTA

Dear Mayor Villaraigosa,
My name is Julissa Acosta, and I am a tenth-grader at Roosevelt High School in Boyle Heights. It is my dream and my major goal to go to college. I would like to become a civil engineer because I like math. I plan to attend Brown University in Rhode Island; I look forward to exploring another part of the country.

I know that to accomplish my goals I will have to work hard and get good grades so that I can go to college on scholarships. When I graduate, I look forward to coming back to Los Angeles and buying a house, where I will live with my mom.

Los Angeles has many wonderful things to offer. There are so many different places to visit and explore, including the mountains and the beach—I would love to learn how to water ski.

Los Angeles is important to me because this is where I have grown up, and this is the place where my whole family lives. L.A. is a good place to live, but it could be a much better place. It would be really helpful if you could make these things happen:

1. Build more high schools in East L.A.
2. Create more jobs for teens
3. Clean the streets
4. Get rid of the graffiti
5. Plant new trees all over the city

These are some of the things that I know would create a better L.A. I promise that if you give consideration to my dreams for Los Angeles, I will succeed in my dream of going to college.

Thank you for reading my letter, and I wish you good luck as mayor.

Sincerely,

Julissa Acosta

Entering New Territory: *Student Editorial Board*

ABOUT THE AUTHORS

JULISSA ACOSTA

My name is Julissa Acosta, and I'm currently a fifteen-year-old sophomore at Roosevelt High School. I am a cheerleader, and I love to dance. I'm a responsible girl who takes AP classes and is dedicated to her education.

ALEXANDER AMADOR

I spend most of my time with my girlfriend, Marisela, or cruising down Soto and Eighth streets on my low-rider Schwinn bicycle with some of the homies. For me, school is a struggle.

FABIOLA AVILA

I am a senior at Roosevelt High. I'm a friendly person who likes to have fun with my family and friends, and I am always myself around everyone. My friends say I am obsessed with Tinkerbell—but I don't care!

GABRIELA BAUTISTA

I like to make people laugh. I love animals and hope to be a veterinarian. I am studious and participate in many school activities.

VIRIDIANA BERNAL

My name is Viridiana Bernal. I am a junior at Roosevelt High School. Even though I'm almost at the end of the road, I don't know who or what I want to be. There are places to go, things to explore, and people to know.

DAVID BLANCARTE

I am the abused and confused, eternal light diffused, God's mental thoughts suffused, in a little sage bemused, the truth succumbed to seclusion, in search of reality but tangled in delusion, as I face faceless fatality.

ISSAMAR CAMACHO

Issamar Camacho was born in Los Angeles in 1990. She lives with her mother and two younger siblings. She wants to be a civil rights lawyer and is involved with a civil rights organization called BAMN (a coalition to defend affirmative action, integration, immigrant rights, and the fight for equality: By Any Means Necessary).

EDWIN CERVANTES (E.T.)

My nickname is E.T., and I like all kinds of music; I also like girls and movies. My favorite movie is *Saw*. I'm currently sixteen years old, and I live in Boyle Heights.

EDGAR CONTRERAS

Who am I? At home I am hardworking and serious. At school I am, for the most part, hardworking, shy, and funny. When I am with my friends I am goofy and can't stop telling jokes. Everybody has days when they are sad, happy, or goofy, but I exercise all these emotions in a single day.

CRISTINA CORREA

My name is Cristina Correa. I'm fifteen years old, and I wish I was born in the 1940s.

KRISTOPHER ESCAJEDA

Kristopher Escajeda is an average kid who attends Roosevelt High School. He is known for his odd taste in clothing and his passion for the guitar. In his writing he defines himself with the truth and with the exotic use of colors.

ERIK ESTEVEZ

Born and raised in South Central L.A. Went to high school in East L.A. The one thing I've learned in my seventeen years is that there's always tomorrow, so don't live in regret.

EVELYN FLORES

I am a seventeen-year-old young adult who enjoys swimming. I am practically in love with art, and I spend much of my time drawing. I am sweet but shy and also look very young for my age.

GABRIELA FONSECA

My name is Gabriela Fonseca, and I live in East L.A. with my two annoying brothers. I love reading; my favorite author is Lurlene McDaniel. I want to become a teacher and stay in one place.

JACKELYN GOMEZ

I was born in Boyle Heights in Los Angeles. My mother is a single parent to me and my five sisters and little brother; she is like an older sister to me. I'm a seventeen-year-old senior at Roosevelt High School, and I participated in the 826LA book project because I wanted to practice my writing. My goal is to become a public defender.

JENNIFER GUERRA

I'm sixteen, and I'm always on the move. I love dogs and rock-climbing. I care about my friends. My family is the most important thing in my life (even though I argue with my sister all the time).

MINERVA HENRIQUEZ

My name is Minerva Henriquez, and I attend Roosevelt High

School. I'm a senior, but I'm still confused about what college I want to go to. I love to laugh and joke around with my friends. My passion is helping people and making them as happy as I am.

EDUARDO HERNANDEZ
My name is Eduardo Hernandez. I was born in Guanajuato, Mexico, but was raised in East L.A. I lived in an orange-colored apartment for fifteen years and then moved to the Pink House. I would like to study medicine and travel the world.

KEREN HERNANDEZ
My name is Keren Hernandez, and I'm sixteen years old. I was born in Torreón, Coahuila, Mexico, and I was brought to Los Angeles when I was eight months old. My favorite dessert is ice cream, and I love animals. I hope to become a pediatric nurse.

JESSSICA JUAREZ
Jesssica Juarez is a ninth-grade student in the Humanitas Academy at Roosevelt.

CARINA LOPEZ
I am a proud Mexican who is grateful for every moment of her life. I am a student who wishes and hopes for a better future, and who appreciates all her family's struggles. I want the best for everyone who wishes it wholeheartedly.

EVELYN MARTINEZ
My name is Evelyn. I was born and raised in East L.A., and I'm currently a freshman at Roosevelt. My two favorite pastimes are rappelling and horseback riding. I'm a very outgoing person, and I'm not afraid to say what's on my mind.

JACKELINE MARTINEZ
I am sixteen years old, a junior at Roosevelt, and I love playing sports. I am really friendly and enjoy meeting new people. My dream is for L.A. to be a place of unity.

ESPERANZA MENDEZ
I'm a go-with-the-flow person. I could really come to care about people when I want to, but most of the time I don't pay attention to my surroundings. I like to challenge myself with new things, but if I don't get it, I give up really easy. I'm just an ordinary student who attends Roosevelt High School, and whatever things happen, I keep them to myself or share them with whoever I trust most.

PATRICIA MENDEZ
I like to play soccer, but I'm not on a soccer team. I'm a friendly person, and I love to share experiences with family and friends. I like to hang around with friends who never judge me. After school I spend most of my time in church, learning more about my religion.

My favorite thing is to assist people who need my help; I enjoy making a difference.

YVETTE MORENO

My name is Yvette Moreno. I have always lived in East L.A. I hope that people enjoy my contribution to this book and that the book reaches a wide audience. I am really proud of myself because I never thought my writing might be included in such a project.

CHRISTIAN OLIVA

Christian Oliva was born in Los Angeles and grew up in Boyle Heights. He is a senior, and he's going to college next year. His favorite book is *The Perks of Being a Wallflower* by Stephen Chbosky. Christian thanks his older brother Omar for being such a great influence, being a terrific mentor, and guiding him through life.

DIMAS ORTIZ

I am a Latino kid who likes to play sports and is very friendly.

ARNOLD PRIETO

My name is Arnold Prieto. I am engaged in music, magic, and my karma in life.

ANA RIOS

My name is Ana Rios. I was born on July 6, 1989. I have lived most of my life in West L.A., but a cou-

ple of years ago we moved here to East L.A. I enjoy spending time with my family, and I also enjoy shopping at the mall. I would have to say that singing is my favorite thing to do—actually I think singing is my passion.

ROSALINDA ROCHA

I was born in the barrios of Los Angeles. I'm sixteen, and I'm a student at Roosevelt High School. I'm the youngest of three kids in a family that comes from Mexico. I would like to be a child psychologist when I grow up because I'm good at listening and I like working with kids.

HECTOR RODRIGUEZ

I'm a sixteen-year-old man living in Boyle Heights. I'm just trying to get by without having to worry about getting shot or something. I attend Roosevelt High, and my intentions are to graduate and work on my dream car, a 1968 Chevy Caprice.

JUAN RODRIGUEZ

Juan Rodriguez was born in Los Angeles in General Hospital. He is now a devoted runner and happy team member of L.A. Shadow. He likes to read and wants to learn many things about the world. He would like to thank his loving family for everything they have done for him.

WENDY RODRIGUEZ
My name is Wendy Rodriguez and I'm a seventeen-year-old senior. I love my family and my boyfriend, but most of all I love the Lord, my Savior Jesus Christ. God willing, I will go to college and pursue my education in early childhood development.

ALEJANDRO ROSALES
I have lived in Boyle Heights all my life. I like to listen to music and use the computer all day long. This is the very first time I've written something like this of my own free will. I hope all our readers like our work. Thanks.

MADELINE SALAZAR
Talented, intellectual, courageous, but most of all determined to fight and overcome every obstacle on her path to success. Loves monkeys! And thanks her family for their support and love and will repay them by being an engineer and motivating others to do well in the future.

MARISOL SALGADO
My name is Marisol Salgado. I'm seventeen and have a passion for words, numbers, and science. I'm always willing to try new things and love to help others. I dream of becoming a pediatrician, and I don't like to give up.

MARIA SANCHEZ
I'm sixteen years old. I have a sister and two brothers who I love a lot, as well as my parents. They are the most important thing in my life. However, I also love something else, and that's music. I like classical and modern music. I play the flute in the Roosevelt Marching Band and the trumpet in the All-City Band. My favorite animal is the dolphin.

LADY SEPULVEDA
Lady Sepulveda is an eleventh-grade student in the Humanitas Academy at Roosevelt.

MADELYN TAPIA
Oh many a blunder goes asunder . . . oh . . . I'm writing . . . um . . . I am a Mexican American who is in a school program called Humanitas, and I decided to write a poem for this book. Besides that I am a seventeen-year-old Socrates and Incubus fan devoted to learning.

STEPHANIE VELASQUEZ
Stephanie Velasquez is an eleventh-grade student in the Humanitas Academy at Roosevelt.

SOME WHO HELPED WITH THIS BOOK

These adults helped edit the works contained in this book.

ANNE FISHBEIN is a fine-art and commercial photographer. Her work can be found in the collections of The Museum of Modern Art, the National Gallery of Canada, Musée Niepce, and the Los Angeles County Museum of Art. Perceval Press published her monograph *On the Way Home.* She is represented by Farmani Gallery in Los Angeles and Printworks in Chicago.

MARITA FORNEY teaches ninth- and twelfth-grade English in the Humanitas Academy at Roosevelt High School. She has a master's degree in Liberal Arts from St. John's College. Her strong belief in the power of literature to open minds makes her especially grateful for this opportunity to have our students' words published and read.

OSCAR GARZA is editor-in-chief of *Tu Ciudad/Los Angeles,* an English-language magazine about Latino life and culture in Southern California. His career includes a sixteen-year stint at the *Los Angeles Times* where he held several senior editor positions.

DEAN KUIPERS is the author of the forthcoming book *Burning Rainbow Farm,* and the deputy editor at the weekly newspaper *Los Angeles CityBeat.* He lives in Mar Vista.

GENEVIEVE LEONE has an MFA in poetry-writing from UC Irvine. In addition to writing poetry, she works for Mattel and names toys.

DEBORAH LOWE teaches tenth and eleventh-grade English in the Humanitas Academy at Roosevelt High School. She is a sponsor of Club Respect, Roosevelt's Gay Straight Alliance. Inspiring a passion for reading is her mission.

TAMI MNOIAN is a writer and editor who has recently tried her hand at teaching and music-video directing.

ESTELLE OST is a ninth-grade English teacher in the Humanitas Academy at Roosevelt High School. She works with young people new to the high school experience. After decades of studying, working, and raising a daughter who now attends UCLA,' Estelle has finally achieved her life-long goal of infusing her love of literature into her work with students.

SHERRI SCHOTTLAENDER is a freelance editor who lives in San Diego with her husband Brian and Tallulah Mae, the Wonder Dog. When she's not obsessing about commas and subject/verb agreement, she can usually be found tending her garden or reading a good book.

JACOB STRUNK is a writer and filmmaker. He lives with his cat, Stephen, and a few framed posters in Hollywood, California. He makes films, he tells stories—he has to.

DAVID L. ULIN is Book Editor of the *Los Angeles Times*. He is the author of *The Myth of Solid Ground: Earthquakes, Prediction, and the Fault Line Between Reason and Faith* (Viking, 2004).

DEBORAH VANKIN is a senior lifestyle editor at *Variety*. Her writing has appeared in the *New York Times*, *Variety*, *L.A. Weekly*, and several other national publications.

GAIL WRONSKY is the author of seven books, mostly poetry, the newest of which is *Poems for Infidels* (Red Hen Press). She is Director of Creative Writing and Syntext at Loyola Marymount University and lives in Topanga Canyon.

ACKNOWLEDGMENTS

This book required months of hard work from students, teachers, and 826LA tutors. The participating Roosevelt High School students faced this project with incredible determination—they stayed after school three days a week over three months, even coming in on Saturdays to make sure that their contributions to this book would be the best that they could be. I hope that you are inspired by the honest, insightful, and creative stories in this collection.

On behalf of 826LA, I would like to thank the three English teachers at Roosevelt High School who spearheaded the project, Deborah Lowe, Marita Forney, and Estelle Ost—this book would not have been possible without their dedication. We must also acknowledge the assistance of other Roosevelt High staff: Bernard Terry, Steve Lopez, Susan Anderson, Sonia Herrera, Brian Waldman, Carlos Ramos, Deborah Thompson, and Brendan Schallert. Special mention must be made of principal Cecilia Quemada for her support of teachers and students alike.

With the enthusiasm of our tutors and the hard work of the students, we met an impossible deadline that was dictated by the complicated Roosevelt A-track year-round schedule. Tutors met regularly with students to review numerous drafts of personal narratives, short stories, and poems—drafts that finally came together after intense one-on-one work sessions. The sight of tutor and student, elbow to elbow, working away and discussing ideas, words, plot, character development, and always, the comma, was inspiring to us all.

The 826LA tutors' work was invaluable, and they must all be mentioned here: Adam Baer, Shelby Benson, Rebekah Bradford, Greg Brown, Janelle Brown, Jessica Buzzard, Juliette Carrillo, Laura Chamorro, Darcy Cosper, Jeff Crocker, Amanda Davis, George Ducker, Jason Fischman, Eric Friedman, Tatyana Gelfond, Josh Gronsbell, Julie Gumpert, Sarah Gurman, Brenna Guthrie, Amanda Haskell, Anna Hirsh, Dave Holmes, Danny Hom, Bryan Hurt, Jerry Jaffe, Lindsey Johnson, Herb Jordan, Joanne Kim, Scott Lasker, Sarah Lebo, Genevieve Leon, Matt Markwalder,

Galen Meuer, Nancy Miller, Tami Mnoian, Julius Panoringan, Aashish Parekh, Eve Ann Porinchak, Daniel Roth, Will Richter, Lauren Savail, Bob Self, Robert Shapazian, Meredith Sires, Theresa Sotto, J. Ryan Stradal, Jacob Strunk, Lien Ta, Amy Waldman, Diana Wendling, Sita White, George Wolf, and Xanadu Xero.

The extraordinary student editorial board deserves special recognition for all the work that they did above and beyond writing their own pieces: Gabriela Bautista, Viridiana Bernal, Erik Estevez, Jennifer Guerra, Minerva Henriquez, Eduardo Hernandez, Evelyn Martinez, Arnold Prieto, Marisol Salgado, and Madelyn Tapia.

Thanks must also go to our community editorial board—these professional writers and editors volunteered to assist editing the student texts: Oscar Garza, Genevieve Leone, Dean Kuipers, Tami Mnoian, Jacob Strunk, David L. Ulin, Deborah Vankin, and Gail Wronsky. We would also like to express our thanks to Anne Fishbein for her insightful lens, which produced the cover photographs; Michele Perez, for creating the book's elegant design and devoting so many hours to its production; and copy editor Sherri Schottlaender, for always making us look better. Thank you to Claire Smith for her assistance and for shepherding the tutors on this project. I must also mention Lisa Fredsti and Jim Bickhart, who helped me introduce this project to Mayor Antonio Villaraigosa.

Extreme gratitude is due to Mayor Villaraigosa for his heartfelt attention to the Roosevelt students and this book project: Thank you for encouraging us all to dream about the City of Angels, and specifically for supporting the voices of these students, your fellow alumni, and more importantly, our future. I must also acknowledge your staff who work tirelessly to better educational opportunities for all students in Los Angeles.

Lastly, this book would not have been possible without the generosity of Max Palevsky and Jodie Evans, who funded it. Thank you.

I also thank the students for bringing me east and reintroducing me to *nuestro pueblo*.

Pilar Perez
Executive Director
826LA

ABOUT 826LA

826LA helps students, ages 6 to 18, with their writing skills, whether in the realm of creative writing, expository writing, or English as a second language. We offer free drop-in tutoring, after-school classes, storytelling events, and assistance with student publications.

TUTORING IS AT THE HEART OF IT

Our method is simple: we assign free tutors to students so that the students can get one-on-one help. It is our belief that great advancement in English skills and comprehension can be made within hours if students are given concentrated help from knowledgeable tutor-mentors. We also offer tutoring in English as a second language.

FIELD TRIPS

We want to help our teachers get their students excited about writing while also helping students to be better at expressing their ideas. We welcome teachers to bring their classes in for field trips during the school day. A group of tutors is on hand at every field trip, whether we are helping to generate new material or revise already written work. Our most popular field trip is Storytelling & Bookmaking; the entire class works together with our tutors to create a story, along with illustrations, and each student leaves with his/her own book.

WORKSHOPS

Our tutors are experts in all different areas of writing, from comic books to screenplays to science fiction. That's why we're able to offer a wide variety of free workshops to students. One of our favorites so far, "ImagiNation: If I Were King or Queen . . ." allows students the opportunity to create their own country, replete with maps, flags, and laws. Workshops are offered almost every day of the week, so sign up!

IN-SCHOOL PROJECTS

The strength of our volunteer base allows us to make partnerships with Los Angeles–area schools. We coordinate with teachers and go en masse to a school and work with students in their classrooms. For example, if a history teacher at Venice High feels her students could use extra help revising a paper on violence in the Middle East, she could ask 826LA for support from ten tutors for her 2 PM Thursday class. Tutors will arrive, ready to work one on one.

A BUSY SCHEDULE OF EVENTS

A busy schedule of guest speakers, classes, storytellers, and special events keep the building an active place. Please check www.826LA.org for our schedule of events.

For more information, please visit www.826LA.org, or email info@826LA.org.